"Let me help you, Kate," he begged

Katherine closed her eyes as a tear slipped down her cheek. "I can't, Luke," she whispered brokenly, catching her breath in furious reaction to her own loss of control. "You just don't understand!"

"No," he agreed gently, "I don't understand. You know your father is trying to ruin your life, so I don't understand why you won't let me help you."

"You're a stranger!" Kate hurled back uncontrollably. "Why should I trust you! What do you want from me?"

"Nothing," Luke replied softly. "I do, however, want a great deal *for* you. Please, Kate, let me see you again."

And the longing to do just what he asked was almost too great to resist.

AMANDA CARPENTER, who wrote her first Harlequin romance when she was nineteen, was raised in South Bend, Indiana, but now lives in England. Amanda endeavors to enhance the quality of her romance novels with original story lines and an individual style. When she's not writing, she pursues her interests in art, music and fashion.

Books by Amanda Carpenter

AMANDA CARPENTER

the gift of happiness

Harlequin Books

TORONTO • NEW YORK • LONDON
AMSTERDAM • PARIS • SYDNEY • HAMBURG
STOCKHOLM • ATHENS • TOKYO • MILAN

Harlequin Presents first edition December 1988
ISBN 0-373-11127-4

Original hardcover edition published in 1986
by Mills & Boon Limited

CHAPTER ONE

KATHERINE made no attempt to walk quietly down the wide staircase, and her booted heels sounded quite audibly on the polished hard wood. The staircase wound around in a gentle spacious curve. The hall below was large and elegant, and a few well-placed tables stood at certain strategic points throughout its length. Expensive and tasteful ornaments decorated these dainty pieces of furniture, and on the main table, just inside the double front doors, stood a huge bouquet of white orchids. Her eyes saw none of these things as she walked through it all with the easy acceptance of one who lived constantly in such surroundings.

Katherine thought of her father's loyal servant with a curl of her upper lip. Joss had seen her enter the house by the back way, and she was sure that he had already informed her father of this. James—she never thought of him any other way, certainly not as Daddy—would be in a rage, she knew, and this thought pleased her in an angry, despairing way. The sounds of a cheerful dinner party floated down the hall from the very large reception room. The party was formal. James had told her so, with steel in his voice which told her clearly that she could not afford to miss it if she had any inkling of what was good for her.

She was used to his domineering ways. For all her life James Farlough had dictated to her how she should be or act, what she should wear, who she should befriend or snub. But those days were over. She had had enough.

Katherine had gone to the best private schools that

her father's millions could buy, and had been kicked out of many for her wild and reckless behaviour. It hadn't mattered. The Farlough money merely bought her entry into others. It was all one and the same to her. Nobody had discerned in her a certain recklessness that went beyond mere youthful high spirits.

Her long legs strode unhurriedly towards the sounds that were spilling out from the end of the hall, a flash of what might have been amusement appearing in her eyes and almost as quickly disappearing again. She had not bothered to change after her strenuous horse ride, and there was dust on her black, knee-high boots. She had on tight, faded jeans that were tucked into them, and she wore a black blouse that was open at a very tanned and slim throat. There was no visible sign of apprehension on her thin, well-proportioned face with its high, angled cheekbones and its strong forehead and chin. Her eyes were brilliant and hard, looking too large for her face and too intense, as if holding too much life in them. Her long and fashionably cut hair held fiery glints, as if a dancing flame hid in the depths of the gleaming chestnut.

She paused just outside the threshold to tie about her throat a long expensive black tie that she had taken the time to fetch from her father's wardrobe. After setting the knot to one side of her throat in a rakish position, she moved with an athletic and arrogant-looking ease to stand poised and framed in the wide, ornate, open doorway. She waited.

There was a general stir, and many of the formally dressed people turned to look at her, a slim and not-very-tall young woman whose stance compelled attention. She broke out of her stillness and slowly started forward, looking neither right nor left and receiving a hazy impression of glitter from various flashy and expensive designer dresses. Spaced among the different colours were areas of tall square-seeming black—the evening suits of the men. More people turned to look, and some moved out of the way as she headed towards the opposite side of the room where a bar was situated with a young uniformed man in attendance behind it. She was terribly hungry, having stormed out with no supper after the terrible quarrel with her father, and her stomach twisted warningly but she paid it no heed. She had lived on her nerves too long to care much about the damage she was doing to her body by neglecting to eat properly. It was just another aspect of her life that didn't really matter any more. A growing silence was taking over the large room full of glittering guests, many of whom were influential and socially prominent. She reached the bar, placed a casual order, and turned on one heel to lazily survey the crowded room.

She was not surprised to see that she was indeed the centre of the room's attention, and she soon located her father with some other man—presumably Lucas Dalton, the guest of honour—coming her way slowly. Reaching behind her, she took up her drink to toss it off in one swallow. It was whisky, neat, and she deliberately held the abominable liquid in her mouth for a long moment, ignoring its burning as she stared into the dark and curiously blank eyes of the tall stranger beside her father. Then she swallowed and cocked an amused and malicious eyebrow at James, looking into his furious and glacial expression mockingly. Every movement was intended, every expression calculated on her part. She was playing a dangerous game with fire.

James was looking particularly frightening, she noted, and was vaguely surprised to find that it scarcely mattered to her. He had always cowed her into submission before. The moment stretched out in the awful silence as father and daughter stared at each other. The one figure held a curiously menacing stance in his ageing and yet still powerfully built body while the other, young and a little fragile yet taut-looking and haughty held a restless energy in check, and possessed an unconscious power that was all her own. She was unaware of how her seemingly careless pose somehow conveyed an overpowering rage tightly suppressed. The dark stranger watched the two, his eyes penetrating and intelligent.

Then the still scene shifted and James began to move across the floor again towards his daughter. Katherine turned her head away as if uninterested, while she gave the bartender another low-voiced order. Another whisky was placed before her and she picked it up to cradle it in her long slim fingers. She knew her father disliked her to drink spirits, and she knew that he was quite aware of how she disliked whisky. It was a deliberate taunt on her part, a subtle flaunting of independence that was fuelling his anger at her impertinence. He didn't care whether the liquor was bad for her or not, she realised cynically. He just didn't want to see her drunk at one of his parties.

'Darling,' said James indulgently. Only she knew how dangerous that endearment was, coming from him in that light tone of voice. 'You're quite late. We have all eaten supper already. I can't think how you forgot.' Sarcasm dripped from his well-modulated tone, and there were a few snickers. The dark man looked from one to the other of the Farloughs frowningly but remained silent. 'Yet surely Joss informed you that the party was formal?'

'Oh, yes, James,' she purred sweetly, 'I didn't forget.' She flicked an indifferent hand at the tie at her throat. His eyes hardened as he recognised it and his lips thinned. 'He did say that it was black tie.' There were more laughs at this as she affected a droll tone and expression.

James assessed the situation quickly, taking an experienced and coldly comprehensive glance around him at his guests. The ages of the people present were varied, as were the different professions and interests. Most of the men and women were now eyeing Katherine with amusement and interest. His daughter was wildly popular, something he had encouraged, and she had a reputation for eccentricity and uniqueness that would be enhanced, not destroyed by tonight's behaviour. He had in the past helped her out of various scrapes and scenes with an indulgence and a complete awareness of how each one had built up her reputation. He'd hardly ever scolded her for any of her past misdemeanours, for the reputation that Katherine had built up was very advantageous to him. People flocked around the girl's notoriety like flies to honey. After tonight, tales would be circulating throughout the district about the Farlough girl, a character and a positive must for a lively party. He saw too that she had judged the situation much as he had, and only they knew of the dark undercurrent involved in this public exhibition. She had never dared to rebel in the past. Now they were locked in a duel of personalities, the outcome of which was the control of her life.

'Come now,' he said, sounding fond. Only they knew how false that was. 'Enough about tonight, my dear.' For now, she read in his light eyes. Only for now. 'I want you to meet my guest of honour.' He turned and clapped the man by his side on the back with a great show of joviality. 'Luke, I've been very anxious for you to meet my naughty daughter, Katherine. Katherine, my good friend Luke.'

'Ah, yes,' she drawled, and her father stiffened into a terrible tension. She looked the man up and down, ignoring his outstretched hand. 'So you're the wonder boy?'

she asked, smiling to take some of the sting out of her
words. It was an insincere smile, and she knew that she
hovered dangerously on the borderline of rudeness. The
whisky had given her courage, bolstering her recklessness, however, and she didn't regret her actions. She
wouldn't, she knew, until later. 'Quite a . . . real estate
expert, aren't you? Or is it the stock exchange, dear?'

They were still the focal point of curiosity and
everyone was listening with an avid and sickening
attention. She could feel her father's rage pulsing
underneath his bland and smiling exterior, murderous
and directed towards her. She knew that she was
losing everything important in life, and that her
father's ruthless domination would probably eventually
destroy her completely. She had been abominably and
unforgivably rude to a virtual stranger, and had
probably just made an enemy of an important and
powerful man. The knowledge was deep in her large,
proud eyes as she looked up to meet the eyes of the
stranger she had insulted.

She got one of the biggest shocks of her life. Luke
Dalton was fairly tall, taller than most men in the
room at least, and well built, with the controlled
stance of an athlete. His shoulders were widely
proportioned; his slim hips were encased in expensive
black material which hugged them closely. His legs
were long and muscled, and his hands had a corded
strength sewn into their large bones. But what she was
noticing were his eyes.

His face was harshly moulded, two deep grooves
cutting down the sides with dark, heavy brows, level
and direct. She got a hazy impression of a lean
attractiveness, but that didn't matter. His eyes were
what mattered. They were a deep, clear grey. They
stared into her as if looking into her soul, searching
her green orbs intently. There was a keen intelligence

in that glance, and curiously no anger, and something else, that she couldn't have defined if her life had depended on it. It looked like sympathy, but it couldn't be that, she surmised. The man doesn't know me, she thought. As far as he's concerned, I'm a spoiled brat. That's good. I need to further that impression.

Whatever else she saw in his eyes, she realised that this man was powerful in a way that was different from anything that she'd ever experienced before. He was to be reckoned with.

'Hotels,' he said gently, and she shivered from that dark gentleness. It was like nothing her father could produce. 'I own hotels. I've been fortunate, but a great deal of it has been hard work.'

'Just so,' she murmured and suddenly, devilishly, quite for the sheer hell of it, she threw back her head and laughed. This, more than anything, shocked her father and the few who had been able to detect the anger waves between the two Farloughs. She stood there, amid the ruin of her young life and more than a hundred guests, and laughed with her head thrown back. Her rich hair rippled over her shoulder like a flame and her laughter rippled over the heads of the guests. 'And what,' she asked mischievously, with an extravagant gesture of one slim, brown hand, 'would *I* know about work, Mr Dalton? Nothing, I quite assure you! It sounds so novel!' Moving forward, she tucked her hand into the crook of his arm, felt the immense strength of him, and began to turn him away from her father. She started to walk with him, pacing her steps to his longer ones and he moved with her, surprisingly compliant. 'Why don't you tell me a little about it, Mr Dalton, while we circulate among the guests? Tracy, that is a charming little frock—— Why, he*llo*, Mrs White, so nice to see you, too! ... And Timmy, oh dear, Tim*othy* now ... heavens it is quite a crush, isn't it? . . . And will it rain, do you think? . . .'

Two people, one with a fire in her hair and eyes, the other with a deep darkness, circulated, and dozens of eyes were drawn to them.

God! to escape out through the large, open french windows was what she needed, she found as she slid stealthily out through a heavy curtain when a small orchestra started playing and dancing was about to resume. She had the shot of whisky, as yet untouched, and she skirted a few bushes, heading through several trees to get beyond sight of the house, unaware that she was being followed. She found a spot in a small clearing and dropped under a tree that stood at the top of a gentle slope that led down to the Kentucky river. The water glinted gently under the glow of the new moon. It was quite easy to see in the soft light that suffused the summer land, and the shadows from the trees were a soothing grey. It was warm, and a slight breeze fanned her face, lifting up her hair and idly blowing it across her cheeks as if to play some light trick on her. She brushed it away absently and stared at the amber liquid in her hand. Suddenly she drank it, not bothering to hide her shudders in the cloaking darkness. It hit her tender throat and burned her stomach. She looked unseeingly in front of her.

Her depression was deep and total. At the age of twenty-one, Katherine Marie Farlough had what most people would consider everything in the world. She was young, beautiful, and the daughter of a very rich and distinguished man. What more could she possibly want or conceivably need?

'*God!*' The word was almost wrenched from her, and she lifted her hand to throw the expensive glass far away, but her hand dropped instead to the ground and pounded it in one furious thump on a hard root that stuck up out of the grass. The word carried all the anguish and torment that she held in her bleeding heart. It held all her despair.

She wouldn't win, she knew. She was not a match for her father's vindictiveness and thwarted spite. She was stronger than most people, yes, but she couldn't stand up to him any more. After a lifetime, it would appear that James Farlough was about to break his daughter.

All her life, James had overshadowed any decision that she had made. At one time, when she was very young, she had been coaxed into thinking that her father was the most romantic father in the world, in spite of the fact that he more often than not forgot her birthday and his visits to see her at boarding-school had been infrequent at best. Every time he had come to see her, though, he had showered her with lavish presents, charmed her with his white and easy smile, and had taken every one of her childhood friends' hearts away for ever. All her teachers had thought that she had everything a little girl could dream of and were at a loss to explain the oddly adult look and pervasive sadness that sat deep in little Katherine's eyes. She had quickly seen with the wisdom of the very young that her father's carelessness showed indifference and his charm hid a calculated manipulation.

As she had grown older, missing her mother in a vague and formless way having never known her, James's role had become more active until his desires and wishes had been forced to take precedence in her young life. She graduated from school and was presented to Kentucky's finest immediately, taking that polite but snobbish horse society by storm. Of course she could ride like a devil bent on destruction. She played tennis with an awesomely competitive spirit—and as a result hardly ever lost a game. She was quite superb with the subtle verbal cut or witticism. She had attended the very best parties at her father's insistence and had dated only the socially prominent young men of whom he approved. More often than not these men were in some way connected with her father's business interests, again at his insistence.

Gradually the awareness had come over her that she was little more than a pawn, a useful tool in her father's life, that her own happiness meant little or nothing to the man who controlled it so ruthlessly. She was a very intelligent girl, too intelligent to be used and never suspect the truth, but just how little she meant to him she hadn't realised until she'd been involved with a young boy some four years back. Her father had broken things off with a callousness that had been shocking. He had ignored her tears and pleading and had finally rounded on her with a coldness and a fury that had left her considerably shaken and in no doubt as to his own feelings. The boy was unsuitable and from a nondescript family background. He was not going to allow her to make a stupid fool of herself over a mere nobody. He had better things for her to do, and more important people to impress. He had said finally, that if she didn't like it, tough. His word was law in his own home. Her feelings didn't enter into the picture.

After he had left her room, two silent tears had crept down her still white face as the last of any adolescent yearnings or hopes had died a final death. She had never gone through any adolescent defiance, although she had been provoked into somewhat wild behaviour to see if James really cared or not. He hadn't, she had seen, as he'd paid for her extravagances and pulled her out of escapades, all with a contemptuous little smile and a careless indulgence that had bewildered her completely. She had never been able to ruffle him, not even with the most outrageous actions and had always submitted to his infrequent demands with a stunned and docile acceptance.

That late-night scene had left her with a badly scarred heart and a determination never to be vulnerable again. And she had lived up to that determination, never letting any of the men she'd been told to go out with close enough for a deep relationship. She'd built up a wall of brittle gaiety and sarcastic remarks. As a result most people laughed at her jokes and at the same time kept enough distance to protect themselves from her caustic tongue and penetrating observances.

It was not that James actually hated her. She was simply no better than the rest of the world around him. His easy charm was a tool that he used to manipulate everyone, and his vindictiveness when thwarted had been shown to her at various times during her life. She had seen him set out to accomplish the ruin of a businessman who had backed out of a promise he'd made to James. She had seen him completely demolish the composure of a waiter in an exclusive restaurant in Louisville. The waiter, she'd later learned, had been fired. And the servants at home would never think of disobeying an order from James, she knew. There were examples from the past that somehow reached the ears of every new employee of how it was quite impossible to get hired again when one had been dismissed by James Farlough.

Her father's one love was power. He actually derived enjoyment from his maliciousness, she had discovered, and he would not hesitate to wield situations to his advantage. Katherine, never having stayed at one school very long and having her eyes open to the shallow and petty nature of the spoiled group that she associated with, was quite alone. She had no true friends.

To be accurate, she had never felt the need for any friends, since the people she knew were not necessarily people that she respected. And also she was a very reserved person under all her apparent extroversion. She did not open herself up to anyone.

Her thoughts turned to an incident the week before which had set the torch of rage to the dry timber in her starved mind, kindling a flare that threatened to consume her.

'Darling,' James had said carelessly, kissing her on the forehead and laughing at her slight flinch, 'I need you to be nice to someone, a Luke Dalton to be exact.'

'No,' she had said flatly, surprising herself and him. 'You were just cursing the man to hell last month. I won't be a part of any of your plots.'

'Cut out the hysterics!' he had commanded coldly. 'All I want you to do is to make him like you and go out with him for a while.'

'I said no. I'll go out once in a while with your business associates but not your enemies. I can't understand you!' she had exploded suddenly. 'You certainly encourage hypocrisy! How can I forget that you called him an "upstart bastard"? Or had the expletive slipped your mind? Perhaps you changed your mind?' She had swung out of her chair in agitation. 'No, you're planning something, and I don't want any part of it, d'you hear? I *know* how your mind works!'

He had grabbed her shoulders and had shaken her hard, throwing her away from him afterwards. She'd fallen into a chair, frightened, and had watched him with large green eyes as he towered over her in a rage. 'You'll do as I say,' he grated while his eyes burned a warning into hers. 'I don't want to hear anything more about it! Don't defy me, Katherine. You aren't strong enough, and I won't put up with it. Not now, not ever!

Not from you,' he flicked her with a hurting finger, 'nor anyone else.'

It was the start of what turned out to be a very grim battle, one that did not deal with just one incident in her life, but instead the whole fate of her personality. She knew that James would try to break her if she seriously defied him, and yet this knowledge somehow strengthened her resolve to try and escape from the absolute hold he had over her entire life.

Well, she thought grimly as she hunched over drawn-up knees, she certainly knew how to ruffle him now. She had angered him beyond any point that he'd ever been with her, and she shivered as she realised that full retribution would soon come down on her head. She had gone to the point of no return, and beyond. She was now at the point where she didn't care if she lost this battle of wills or not. She had a good idea of what could happen to her, but something deeply hidden and incredibly stubborn had awoken in her. She had grown up in some way in the past few days. James could possibly break her, but he would never, ever bend her to his will. Not ever again.

She thought of the conversation that she'd overheard as she had been right outside her father's office the day before, the Friday when she had realised that she would never submit to her father again.

'. . . You're damned right, I'm going to get it! I still can't believe that he managed to get to Parson and make a bid in private and that Parson accepted! It's incomprehensible! That sonofabitch bit off more than he can chew, when he interfered with me. I would've outbid any price that Dalton could have paid on the open market for those water-front storehouses, and how he gulled Parson into selling for a lower price, I don't know. In secret!'

'Well, you were going to do the same if you'd had

the chance, weren't you?' came back the tones of his executive vice-president, Earl Jacobi. Katherine had stopped at the sound of Dalton's name and, knowing what her father had asked of her, and knowing that the party on Saturday was ostensibly to introduce Dalton to Kentucky society, she had listened without knocking.

'That's beside the point. Are you coming to the party tomorrow night?' Her father had suddenly sounded amused.

'You know I am. What I can't figure out, though, is what you have in mind, James. I know it's got to be something, since I've never seen you so full of hatred for someone before! And now you're opening your arms to Dalton in welcome.'

'Only to place the knife in his back, my boy. Katherine is very beautiful, is she not?'

'You know she is,' Earl replied deeply. 'She's one of the most beautiful women I know.'

'A piece that Dalton might fancy? I hope she's able to put him off guard. He might even want to marry her, if I can get her to be nice enough, although that could develop quite naturally without my help. He's a handsome bastard.'

'James! You wouldn't let Katherine marry a man you hated, would you?' Earl asked him, aghast.

'Oh, no. I'd call an end to it before that. All I need is for her to put him off guard, to stall for time while I devise the best way to ruin him. Hell, she can sleep with him for all I care, but she'll never get tied up with him—she's too useful to me in other ways. We need those warehouses, Earl. I've been waiting for such an opportunity for years! I want to hurt Dalton; I want him ruined! I've had that infernal devil on my mind for the past eighteen months, ever since he began causing us more trouble than a nest of hornets—whatever possessed Parson to sell to Dalton is beyond me . . . doesn't he know that Dalton wants to tear down those precious warehouses of his and put up a hotel there? . . . Have to stop him before he gets that far, may not get another chance at water-front warehouses for another ten years . . .'

Katherine had forgotten why she had come to her father's office, and had crept away, sickened in the very centre of her heart. There had been no one around, since her father's secretary had been at lunch, and she'd thought to catch him by surprise for some reason or another, but it didn't matter any more, not after what she had just heard. The conversation had hit her when her self-esteem had already been lamentably low, and reverberations of shock kept running through her system.

So that's why he wanted me to be nice to Dalton! she had thought furiously, running one trembling hand through her hair. And I had assumed that it was a lighter, social matter, never suspecting how deep his animosity really ran! She had driven home, for once not appreciating the lush green pastures of high summer as the phrases of the overheard conversation still echoed in her ears, lashing the words at herself in a frenzy of rage.

'I'll see you in hell before I ever let myself be used, like some piece of meat to be sold for the highest price!' she'd thrown at him only that afternoon in a blazing fight.

'I'll see you in hell,' she whispered now into the darkness, remembering how he had struck her over one ear with one closed fist. He'd taken care not to mark her face, she realised dully, because of the party that evening. It was a frightened whisper now, though, not a bit like the brave-sounding words she had flung at him earlier like a challenge. Her own smaller fist closed over the whisky glass in an uncontrolled spasm and, weakened by the blow on the exposed root, the hard roundness fragmented. She felt the several pieces shift and, before she could react to relax her grip, she felt a sharp, penetrating pain as a jagged corner bit into her flesh. A warm trickle of blood flowed from the gash in her palm, dripping into the grass. After the first hiss of pain, she dropped the bits of broken glass and watched the flow with interest. The pain was clean and sharp, not at all like the muddy mess of her own emotions, and she appreciated the fact. She almost enjoyed the stabbing throbs that were hitting her now. It was clearing her head.

'Quite a nice little escape from the crush inside,' a deep voice drawled from her left. She turned quickly, seeing a dark shadow that was strolling her way from under the cover of the trees.

'Fresh air, and all,' she replied flippantly as the shadow materialised into the bulky shape of Luke Dalton. She dropped her hand to her side, a little way away from her to avoid staining her clothes.

'Er, yes,' he sounded amused. Dropping down on the ground beside her a few feet away on her right, he asked lightly, 'Are you hiding?'

'Good heavens,' it was her turn to play amusement, 'dear boy, from what?'

'Who knows, apart from yourself? he asked in return, casually. 'From your father's anger, from me, from your own rudeness—you were, you know, quite rude. From the party and all those well-dressed, snickering women. Can you answer it?'

Katherine sensed a certain tension in the dark figure that seemed suddenly too close. She threw back her head and laughed, this time in genuine amusement. 'Do you really think that I care about those stuffy, snobbish hags in there?' she asked contemptuously.

'Half will go home determined to invite me to their next party, and the other half will go and gossip bitchily about me at their next intimate conversation with their twenty closest friends! It doesn't concern me, I assure you, in the slightest!'

'Honey,' he said cynically, 'I'm quite sure of that! You've really gauged the reactions in there well, haven't you? Should I think of you with admiration?'

'I don't care what you think,' she said bleakly. There was silence.

He was leaning back a little, half in and half out of shadow, both hands linked around one knee. 'I can't think,' he said mildly, 'just why you would be in such an abominable temper, unless you are a shrew by nature? Or perhaps it was that excellent meal that you so deliberately missed? Do you get a kick out of trying to ruin dinner parties?'

'Ruin?' she said tonelessly. She was beginning to tremble from the lack of food since she hadn't eaten all day. 'I don't ruin parties, Mr Dalton, I add colour. Ask any hostess around here.' The bitterness, tasting like gall, was appallingly apparent.

He asked suddenly, harshly, 'Why do you do it? Why are you doing it? Why make a spectacle of yourself if you feel so bitter about it, Kate? What makes a person like you tick?'

'What difference does it make to you, Mr Dalton?' she countered, measured and cold. Inside she was beginning to feel frightened. She was trying her hardest to make the man hate her, to send him as far away from herself and her father as possible, and after all her rudeness in the middle of what was for him a very important social event, here he was in the dark talking to her! She would try harder. 'For future reference, the name is Katherine to my friends. You may call me Miss Farlough.'

'You are missing your supper, aren't you?' he commented calmly, ignoring her little speech.

She lost her temper. 'Go to hell, Dalton. Just stay out of my life, will you? Go and crawl back under whichever rock you came from and leave me alone!' She felt ridiculously close to tears and clenched her hands into fists. A fresh and frighteningly full spurt of blood gushed from her right palm. The grass beneath her fingers was wet and slick. She didn't care. She really didn't care.

'You are such a little bitch. Where did you get such viciousness from—your father?' He leaned forward, putting one hand down to support himself as he talked. 'You strike out with no provocation at all—what the hell . . .?' He put his hand to his face, and then shifted fast from the tree's shadow to peer at his hand. 'My God,' he breathed, and reached out, quicker than a snake, and grabbed her wrist to jerk it up none too gently. 'That's your blood! What have you done to yourself, you stupid fool?' Not able to see her hand but able to feel its slickness, he pulled her across the ground until she too was out of the shadow, and he stared at her hand that was still clenched tight in a fist. Dark liquid was smeared all over, and it dripped from between her closed fingers. 'What did you do to yourself?' he snapped, shaking her hand. 'Open your fingers and let me see!' His reaction was one of fear, but she misconstrued the rather violent tone of voice as anger and she shrank away from him. He swore under his breath at her silence, and then tried again. 'Come on, Kate, open your hand and let me see it,' but she was not paying attention to his words, and he attempted to pry her hand open with his long, strong fingers. The blood made his grip slip and she doggedly gritted her teeth from the pain, and kept it closed.

And, suddenly the sickening tension that had been with her for far too long snapped and she turned on him in a fury, swinging her free hand up and slapping him hard across the cheek. 'Leave me alone,' she enunciated clearly and precisely. 'I do not, repeat, do not want or need any help from you or anybody else!' She could not tug her hand free and she wrenched hard to catch him off guard, gasping with the pain that shot up her arm. 'Damn you to hell, let go of me!' His hold slipped, and she was free. She whirled, took a step, and then collapsed under a weeping willow tree on that balmy, gentle summer night.

CHAPTER TWO

SOMETHING firm and smooth was under her cheek. It also moved up and down regularly, and when she opened her eyes the moonlight illuminated the dark sleek hair and firm jaw of the man so close to her. Her head lay on Luke Dalton's shoulder, and he was carrying her towards the house. Her hand, which throbbed painfully, was wrapped up and tied with something. She looked at it incuriously; the red material had once been a handkerchief. 'It's quite ruined,' she commented conversationally, indicating her hand.

'Shut up.'

'Now who is being rude?' she asked. 'Put me down, I can walk.' He didn't bother to answer this directive, and she wriggled experimentally. The jaw tightened and so did the arms around her. She could tell he was angry. The set of that jaw was very expressive, even in the dark.

'I said, shut up,' he replied pleasantly. Katherine did not appreciate his tone. After walking a few more steps, he continued as if goaded, 'I have never met a more obstinate, stupid, idiotic person in my entire life. I've never seen a more spoiled, rude and selfish brat. You surpass belief!' The moonlight, until now leaving most of his face in shadow, seemed to be caught in the glitter of his eyes which were flashing with rage. 'Your father should have taken his belt to you years ago——'

She merely closed her eyes and her mind to this low-voiced and furious tirade.

She had given up. All the fight and all the anger had

drained away, leaving an emptiness that she felt would probably never be filled. There was nothing inside, no wellspring of joy from merely being alive, no hate or resentment for her father, no rebellion. There was simply a vacuum, an ache where something had once been, a pit filled with a weary boredom and a desire to sleep. She wanted nothing more than to go to sleep.

It was, however, impossible. As they neared the house and the light that spilled out from every open window, the dark strong figure carrying her spoke. 'Where can we go to escape the guests?'

She didn't answer right away. 'Around the back,' she finally told him as his grip on her tightened. 'We can get into the kitchen from there.'

He altered his steps to take them round the corner of the house. They reached the back door, and he hesitated. 'Do you feel like you could stand for a moment?'

She flashed him a speaking look and remained silent. He put her down carefully and kept one arm around her waist as he tried the door handle experimentally. It was unlocked. He pushed it open and took care to help her up the few steps and into the house. The large kitchen, though full of light and somewhat cluttered from party glasses and trays, was luckily, if temporarily deserted.

He looked around swiftly. 'All right,' he said, leading her to the double sink. 'Let's have a look at your hand.' His tone was expressionless, and she looked at him quickly. What she saw in his stern and uncompromising face made her accompany him without demur.

'Was it deliberate?' he asked evenly. She turned her gaze on him, startled.

'What?'

'I said, was this deliberate?' he spaced out each

word slowly, as he roughly tied a towel around her injured hand, ignoring her gasp of pain. Katherine stared into his eyes. She received another shock as she saw in those dark depths the anger that was submerged, and she began to wonder if she had made a terrible mistake in underestimating this man. She wished that she'd never provoked him to begin with.

His irritation was, she thought, understandable. She had behaved very badly all evening, and she was sure that he saw this incident as a rather childish bid for attention, an attempt to stay in the limelight. She mused on the sudden clarifying insight that he had probably thought she had cut herself deliberately and was about to go back to the party, make a stupid fuss, and try one more time to ruin the gathering. She had acted in a way that would have tried the patience of a saint.

It was the regret she felt for provoking him so that made her answer him relatively mildly. 'If it had been deliberate, I wouldn't have been so clumsy.' She smiled a very small smile, but the first sincere one he had seen, and his grip on her arm loosened. 'The wrist would've been a better target, don't you think? I assure you, if I wished to take such an irrevocable step, no one but no one would find me before it was too late. And,' her eyes twinkled briefly, 'I don't need to stoop to such measures to get attention.'

The anger had faded from his eyes, leaving an expression that she could not define. 'I can believe that,' he murmured. Then, 'Why didn't you mention to me that you were hurt? You sat there for some time, bleeding everywhere.'

Her eyes dropped. 'Does it really matter what my motives were?' she asked quietly. 'Excuse me. I think I'd better get someone to phone the doctor.' She made as if to go, but was forced to halt as his hand tightened on her arm.

'Don't bother. I'll take you to the hospital,' he said crisply, and headed for the door that led to the hallway, pulling her along. She hung back.

'This is crazy,' she protested. 'You can't leave a party when you're the guest of honour. What will people think?'

He sounded amused. 'What do I care? And you are the last person I would expect to care about what others think. Really, Kate, you aren't at all what you seem to be.'

'Katherine,' she corrected him automatically, apparently forgetting that she hadn't wanted him to call her anything except Miss Farlough.

'And do please call me Luke,' he murmured. Reality hit her suddenly, and she stopped dead, refusing to take even one more step and in great danger of being dragged across the floor.

'No!' she said sharply. 'Let go of me, dammit, and go back to your party!' She couldn't afford to have him pay the slightest attention to her. It would destroy her, and very possibly him also. She was beginning to care about that. Surprisingly, against all odds, she liked this man.

'What, for Pete's sake, is the matter now?' he exploded impatiently. 'Good grief, you'd think I had rabies, the way you're acting!' He stared down into her shuttered face, taking in the tight and wary expression in her deep green eyes. She in turn stared into the sternest face she'd ever seen, with implacable eyes and a determined chin. 'Now,' he said softly, 'I am going to take you to the emergency room at the hospital. You are going to go without any fuss. Do you understand me?' She looked into his eyes and her own widened. She just couldn't find any strength for defiance, and she nodded. 'Afterwards,' he continued with scarcely a pause, 'you and I are going to sit down and talk. I'm beginning to think that there's a motive behind all this tonight, and I want an explanation.'

She immediately began to shake her head at this, not trusting his patience if she were to speak, but he ignored this and turned to go out of the kitchen. As his bulk led her slighter frame, two men garbed in uniform appeared in the doorway. One was older with greying hair and a thin face with a tight mouth, and the other was the young man from the bar. The older one headed for them with an exclamation.

Luke cut through the other man's words. 'Miss Farlough has hurt herself, and I'm taking her to the hospital to see if she needs stitches. Would you inform Mr Farlough for us? We shouldn't be too long, I'd imagine.' His tone was impatient as he clearly wanted to get going.

Katherine stared at the grey man bitterly, with hatred. He looked back at her with no expression on his face, but in his eyes there lurked a furtive gleam of malice. She burst out, 'You'll be good at informing James, won't you, Joss? But then,' she added sweetly, 'you've always been good at it before.'

The servant smiled at her slowly, the thin lips stretching tightly over his teeth. Neither noticed the intent expression on Luke's face or the attention that the tall young man was paying to them. 'Of course, whatever you say, Miss Farlough,' Joss murmured politely, the gleam in his eyes belying any subservient attitude. There was a subtle amusement threading his words. Looking at him, Katherine felt an upsurge of hate that left her trembling. She feared this man.

Luke quickly pushed past the older man, pulling her along with him. 'Then be quick about it, man,' he

snapped. 'And stay out of the way.' Joss sent a
suddenly vicious look towards him and Katherine
watched his face as they left the room, her head turned
back. It had been a mistake on Luke's part, she
realised. He had just made an enemy.

The trip to the hospital was brief. 'Come on,' a low-
toned voice sounded right beside her ear. Katherine
stirred lethargically. A hard hand slipped under her
shoulders and she opened her eyes to stare irritably
into the impenetrable ones of the stranger bending
over her. Then she truly woke up and remembered
where she was, and with whom.

'Do me a favour,' she told him, pushing at his arm,
'and don't do me any favours.'

'Cut the act,' the voice sounded amazingly amused.
She stubbornly refused to look up. 'And for heaven's
sake, come on!'

She stood on shaky legs for a minute, with one hand
on the car to see if she needed support. When she
found she could stand unaided, she doggedly set out
for the brightly lit glass doors of the emergency
entrance of the large Frankfort hospital, and ignored
the hand stretched out in an offer of help. The
wooziness was dispelled as she walked, and soon she
found herself almost clear-headed.

They had to wait a bit before a doctor could see
them, and she felt momentarily amused at the odd
sight the two of them must have presented to the
hospital staff and other patients. She was aware of how
incongruous the pair of them must have seemed. Her
long hair was tousled and her jeans dusty, and the man
beside her, so quiet, was as sleek and dark as she was
rumpled and fiery. There could not, she surmised, be
a pair so totally the opposite of each other as we are.
Inexplicably, this made her feel depressed.

Eventually she was sitting on an examination table and a young man in a white coat was attending to her hand. To her immense irritation, Luke insisted on accompanying her to the room and he sat in a chair nearby, watchful and silent. She stared at her arm as the doctor murmured soothing words that she ignored, and she didn't flinch when he gave her an injection. She also watched without blinking or expression as he expertly and quickly gave her wound twelve stitches. While he was bandaging her numbed hand, he told her that the stitches should be taken out in about ten days, and then he gave her some painkillers which she stuffed uncaringly into her pocket. She was unaware of a dark gaze that noted her reactions, and that never left her tired face. She stood indifferently as the bill was settled, but gave a start at a sudden hand on her shoulder.

She looked back at Luke as he stood watching her, absent-mindedly rubbing a thumb along the sharp bone of her shoulder-blade.

'When did you last eat?' he asked, suddenly. Her eyes slid away from his as she shrugged. 'When?' he repeated. 'This morning? Yesterday?'

She didn't answer but merely watched the ground mulishly. A hand propelled her towards the door. 'Let's go,' he said impatiently.

As Luke headed the car out on one of the major roads, she protested, 'This is the wrong way.' He made no reply, but kept on driving. She sat up and watched closely, wondering what this man was up to. She soon found out as he pulled into the car park of a twenty-four-hour restaurant, and she slumped with resignation when he swung into an open space. She had begun to suspect that once Luke Dalton had set his mind to something, there was little on this earth that could stop him.

He said briefly, and not ungently, 'Get out,' and did

so himself. There was nothing else for her to do but the same.

'Do you know,' she said acidly, 'that you are the most obstinate and odious man I've ever had the misfortune to meet?'

He laughed as if he were delighted, and held open the door for her to pass inside. She went by him shakily, the picture of his white teeth gleaming and the laugh lines pronounced as he'd thrown back his head imprinting itself on her mind. She folded her arms tightly across herself as they waited to be seated.

When they had both slid into the booth, the waitress came to take their orders. Katherine, when asked, contrarily said that she wanted nothing. As the waitress blinked at this bald statement and Luke frowned, she turned her head to stare out of the window indifferently. She heard Luke's low voice giving an order for two cups of coffee and a large breakfast of scrambled eggs and ham with toast. He waited until the waitress had disappeared and then turned to her.

'Kate. Kate!' She looked around coldly. He was, again, furious. 'You can be as rude as you like to me. I can take care of myself. But that waitress has a job to do, and you're not making it pleasant for her!'

Two steaming cups of coffee were brought and she stirred a little cream into hers absent-mindedly. 'So what?' she asked carelessly. 'I'm nothing to her, and she's nothing to me. If anything, I'm a nuisance to be forgotten when I walk out of that door. What difference does it make how I act? Who really gives a damn in the long run?' One corner of her mouth quirked humourlessly, and she set down her spoon to cradle her coffee cup with two cold hands, awkwardly cuddling her injured one as close as she could to the warmth. 'I'm a realist, Lucas.'

'No, you're not,' he observed, leaning back in his seat and scrutinising her. 'You're a cynic, and do you know what cynics are? They're disillusioned and hurt romantics. Who's hurt you, Kate? Who has hurt you so badly that you lash out at the world in general, and you don't care if you're hurt or not? You wouldn't even care if you were to die tonight, would you? It just doesn't matter, does it?'

'How many times do I have to tell you?' she hissed at him in a sudden fury, desperate to stop the flow of truth coming from his lips. 'The name is Katherine, do I have to spell it?'

'Oh, you've made yourself quite abundantly clear, my dear,' he replied mildly. Then he shifted his long, powerful body to sit forward, and his eyes captured hers. He was deadly serious now, and she shrank back in her seat as if to try and escape from his compelling eyes. 'I want some answers, Kate. I want some answers to some very uncomfortable questions. Why the scene tonight? You were very deliberate in everything that you did, even down to this stupid persistent rudeness you insist on inflicting upon me! You deliberately set out to provoke your father into fury, and you deliberately set out to try to make an enemy of me, interestingly enough after I had to listen to your father tell me time and time again how much he would have liked me to get to know you better! Why?' His voice had grown softer and softer as he talked, and this somehow enhanced his determined expression. He frightened her, for he seemed so ruthless. He was, after all, no better than her father.

She dropped her eyes so that he could not see the expression in them. 'What difference does it make?' she asked bitterly.

'Stop parroting that stupid defeatist phrase at me!' His words hit her like a bullet and she flinched openly.

'It makes a world of difference! You were so alive tonight!' he exclaimed in impotent fury, capturing her uninjured hand and squeezing the thin bones until she looked up with a yelp of pain. 'You fairly vibrated with rage, and your eyes glowed with more life in them than any of the other colourless saps at that party! Where did it all go, Kate? Was it an illusion? Do you perform best in front of an audience? Was that vibrant laugh a fake after all? Answer me!'

Tears spilled over on to her cheeks at his low, intense words, and they ran down her face. 'Shut up!' she hissed furiously, jerking her hand away to wipe at her eyes roughly. 'Just shut up, will you? You don't know a thing, you don't know one damn thing!'

He sat back, strangely mild now as he watched her glare at him with rage. 'Then why don't you explain things to me?' he asked her gently, not taking his eyes from her face.

The intensity of the murmured exchange was dispelled when the waitress brought the breakfast to the table. Luke motioned for her to place the meal in front of Katherine, and she did so hesitantly. Katherine smiled up at her and thanked her quite nicely. The little waitress, a bit startled, murmured a bemused welcome in return and then hurried away to bring them more coffee. With new steaming cups in front of them and the tantalising smell of the freshly cooked food in front of her, the waitress left and they were again alone.

'Thank you,' said Luke, smiling at her faintly. She looked with some reluctance away from the food, for her stomach was beginning to twist hungrily.

'For what?' She picked up her fork clumsily and attempted to spear a piece of ham. He took her knife and fork away from her and cut up the meat into bite-sized pieces.

'For being so nice to her. The waitress, I mean. There, try to eat that now,' he murmured, and pushed the plate back to her. She dug in heartily. He waited in silence until she had cleared away every bit of the eggs and ham and started on the toast. 'Feeling better?'

She nodded unsmilingly, the look in her eyes tentatively friendly. She didn't feel quite so shaky.

'Feel more like talking?' he asked carefully, gauging her reaction.

'Can I give you some advice?' she said suddenly, urgent. He raised one eyebrow in question. 'Whatever you do, wherever you go, don't, absolutely do not trust my father. Ever.' She wiped her mouth and looked at him. He was sitting very still. 'He is a snake, a viper. He would just as soon bite off your hand as thank you, if you were to give him something to eat. He doesn't like you. You've got in his way by buying those water-front warehouses, and he doesn't take kindly to interference. He hates you, Luke, and would like to see you destroyed.'

Incredibly, he smiled. She stared into his face with consternation. She saw that smile and began to regret what she had just said.

'Forget it,' she muttered, sliding her eyes away and picking up a piece of toast. She began to know a real fear. What if Luke was already so friendly with her father that he would perhaps tell him what she had said? She knew James well enough to be afraid of the consequences, should he hear of this indiscretion. He was angry enough as it was. 'I don't know what I'm talking about.'

'Quite the contrary, my dear,' he said quietly. 'You've hit bang on target. You have just confirmed my own suspicions. You've told me nothing new.' She sagged in her seat with relief, and his gaze sharpened on her. 'Did you really think that I could have been so stupid as not to have seen it?' he asked, with a thread of amusement. 'I've been warned by others before you, my dear!'

She stirred at that, and asked him curiously, 'Who warned you about James?'

'Nobody you would know. A tired, worried old man. I think you'd like him.' He studied her reflectively. 'I had my own reasons for coming to the party tonight, and one of them was to see what kind of trap your father planned on springing on me. That he'll try something, I'll bet my eye-teeth. Just what, though, is still a mystery.'

'He's going to try to ruin your business,' she spoke tiredly, propping up her forehead with her ininjured hand. 'It's his speciality—he's quite good at it, you know, having done it before. Just how, I don't know. I overheard a conversation I wasn't supposed to, and I don't think he really knows yet either. But I do know what the trap is supposed to be.'

'Well,' he said unworriedly, 'I think I can handle the business aspect of it. He'll find himself with more than he bargained for, when he takes me on.' Looking at him, and remembering that dark strength she had sensed when she'd first met him, Katherine had no doubt that what he said was true. 'Just what is the trap, by the way?'

'It's me,' she whispered, suddenly ashamed of her father, more so than she'd ever been before. And, she found, she was somehow ashamed of herself, as if her father's unscrupulous intentions in some way reflected on her own character. His eyes narrowed on her in shock, and he leaned forward abruptly.

'What did you say?' he asked tersely. 'I—don't think I heard you quite right.'

She repeated louder, and with infinite bitterness, 'I said it's me.' He sat as one stunned. 'I am the trap.'

CHAPTER THREE

AFTER a moment, he asked, 'Just what in sweet hell were you supposed to do?' His tone was slightly rough. He hadn't moved from his position, and his coffee sat in front of him untouched. Nevertheless, Katherine got the impression that after her bombshell, he had in some way relaxed after that first tense moment of shock. She looked into his eyes and found them comfortingly calm and steady.

She couldn't confess to such a reaction herself. She was shaking again as she realised just what a precarious position she was in. She had opened herself to infinite dangers when she had confessed to Luke her father's intentions. In the midst of her most consuming rage, she had never conceived of such an action. She had merely thought to refuse his demands. Now, in a surprisingly short time she found herself talking to her father's enemy—and a total stranger at that—and aligning herself in what started to appear uncomfortably like a conspiracy. She saw that this was the best way to thwart her father, though, and she couldn't regret telling Luke any of it, even if she would have to suffer the consequences. But she had never confided to anyone as much as she had to Luke. She couldn't understand what had prompted her to tell him everything. All she knew was that she felt better, as if a load had been taken from her shoulders. She felt relieved. At the same time, she knew that this knowledge would most likely send away one of the most attractive men she'd ever met. She liked Luke far too much, and she was glad she had told him, and at the same time very, very sorry.

She stared into her coffee, and drank a little. 'I was to be nice to you.' Flooded with a sense of shame and degradation, she spat out suddenly as if she'd swallowed poison, 'A sound piece of flesh, a prize, a pawn, a lure!' She looked at him as if she hated him, but she wasn't focusing on his face. Her eyes were looking inward. 'I think I'm going to be sick.'

'Kate!' a hiss penetrated the darkness of her thoughts, and her eyes began to focus on the concerned face of the man in front of her. 'Kate! Snap out of it! Come on, look at me. Look at me!' She watched his face, and the anger faded from hers, leaving her eyes dull and lifeless.

She said, a brittle quality in her voice as if something was stretched tight and about to snap, 'Then he was going to play the coup, and destroy you while your guard was down. I don't know what he has in mind. He's going to try to ruin you, I know that. Maybe he would've tried to make me steal something from you, I don't know.' She sighed and straightened in her seat.

'Didn't your feelings come into the matter?' he breathed incredulously. 'Doesn't your father care that his scheme to destroy me could very well have destroyed you too? He was going to use you as much as he was attempting to use me!' A big clenched fist came down on the table with enough force to set the cups rattling in their saucers, and she jumped a mile. People began to look around at them, and he suddenly stood, his face more grim than she had ever seen it. 'Come on,' he said shortly, throwing some money carelessly on the table. 'Let's get out of here!' As they exited the restaurant, she caught a glimpse of a clock and felt shocked. It was almost three o'clock in the morning.

She looked at Luke's harsh face, with grim tough lines running from nose to mouth. He had never looked so hard before, and she was a little afraid of him in this mood. 'I need to get home,' she said quietly as they climbed into the car. 'It's very late, and I'm tired.'

'Why?' he asked briefly, after a silence, and he turned to stare at her very hard. She stared back, puzzled.

'Why, what?'

'Why do you have to go back?' he asked her abruptly. Stunned, she opened her mouth to protest, but he held up one imperious hand to command silence. He took a breath, hesitated, and asked, 'Are you afraid of him?'

Pride fought a brief war with honesty, and the honesty won. After a moment she whispered, 'Yes.'

'Come home with me.' The words were spoken so very quietly that she wasn't sure she had heard him correctly.

'What?' she asked stupidly.

'You heard what I said.'

It was a shock. It was very definitely the most bizarre invitation she had ever received. 'I don't believe you just said that.'

'Why not?' He was being very patient. 'Do you have anywhere else to go at this time of night? Do you really want to go home after all you've just told me? Don't you want a place where you can go and just feel relaxed and unpressured for a while?' There was a pause. 'I have,' he told her gently, 'a housekeeper and an older sister in the house. It wouldn't be just you and me.'

She flushed painfully at the implication in his words and cursed herself for her own lack of poise. It had been just exactly what she'd been thinking of. Silence crept into the closed area of the car as he gave her time to think. She felt her mind whirling crazily as she thought over and over the unexpected chance to escape from the ominous threat of her father's anger, the repercussions of such a drastic move, the possibilities and the dangers. She didn't have any real friends she could depend on. She would not have to face up to her father's wrath or Joss's malice. She could run away.

Then she thought of the motive behind Luke's offer. Why would he make such a spectacular offer to someone he had just met that night? They were virtual strangers to one another. Could it possibly be because he wanted to use her as a pawn to manipulate her father? She was in an agony of indecision and uncertainty. He was sitting beside her so still and quiet. She could not tell what he was thinking after he had made such an offer. Perhaps he regretted it. Then she thought of how pleased her father would be if he were to hear that she had spent the night at Luke Dalton's house, after just meeting him that night. He would think, she thought bitterly, that I was faster than he would've given me credit for.

It was the thought of the danger that she would be bringing to Luke and his home that finally decided her. She knew that it would be too risky to go with Luke because of the erroneous conclusions her father would come to. If she could continue in her original purpose, and repel Luke as rudely and as consistently as possible, then she might be able to demonstrate to James Luke's alienation from the Farloughs. Hopefully, this would throw a dampener on any kind of move that he would plan to make against Luke. She knew that it would be temporary at best, for her father would just try to think of something else, but that was too far in the future to contemplate. She would think

of something else to do when the time came. She
realised that by Luke's silence he was letting her make
up her own mind, and was not making the offer out of
a desire to manipulate her. Otherwise he would be
entreating her to come to his house tonight. She
acknowledged wryly that she was too afraid. She was
afraid of becoming too attached to Luke, and she was
afraid of being the instrument—however innocently—
used to hurt him. She'd never wanted to hurt anyone.

No, to remain unattached, that was the best
course. Staying aloof was the best way to survive,
she had found. It was a lesson that she had learned
from James. She knew that she was too attracted to
Luke for her own good; it would only lead to
disaster for both of them. It was precisely what her
father wanted.

'No,' she said, raising her head. 'I can't. It's just
what he wants, don't you see? Whatever the reason for
me going with you, he would see it as a sign of your
. . . er, being duped, so to speak. That's too dangerous,
for you and for me. Then, you see, he might feel
comfortable enough to try to bring about harm to your
business. No, I want to go home.'

'You don't *want* to go home,' he said astutely,
stirring a little in his seat and sounding—incredibly, to
her mind—regretful. 'You don't need to lie to me,
Kate. You've told me too much for that. You don't
want to go home, you think you have to go home.
What will you do after tonight?'

'I don't know,' she said tiredly. 'I have no
marketable skills. I have no job experience. I could no
more make a bid for independence than a beast, raised
in captivity, could survive in the wild.'

He looked at her, his head at a slight angle, the
curve of his cheek hard. 'If I take you back tonight,
will you promise me one thing?' he asked.

She looked away. 'It rather depends,' she said cautiously, 'on what it is.'

'Would you let me come over tomorrow morning—this morning—and help you try to figure out what your prospects are for the future?' He stared at her, frowning. 'It might even be a good idea if we make James think that we are seeing each other, and lull him into a false sense of accomplishment.'

'Not that!' she cried out sharply. 'It's too dangerous!'

'All right, we won't settle that tonight. But would you promise about tomorrow morning?' He repeated his question patiently, putting his two hands on the wheel of the car and staring at them thoughtfully. They looked graceful, though large and sinewy, and she too stared at them.

After a hesitation and with some foreboding, she assented reluctantly. She was ashamed of her own weakness, for giving in to him when she knew that the best thing was for her to tell him goodbye and good riddance. It was so pleasant, though, not to feel so appallingly alone in the world. And she was so lonely. 'Although why,' she commented absently, wrapped in her own recriminations and doubts, 'you should bother, is beyond me.'

He started the car and backed out of the parking space. 'Is it?' he asked reflectively. She was not paying attention to him and so missed his words. He murmured to himself, 'I've been wondering that, myself . . .'

It was almost four when he let her off in the large double driveway in front of her home. He told her that he would be calling on her around eleven the next morning. They both agreed to go riding or possibly for a drive, to get away from the prying eyes of the servants and to stay away from her father's speculative attention. As she ran lightly up the steps and opened the big front door, she saw a light gleaming from a crack below the closed door of her father's study. At once, a feeling as if she had just walked into a pit of darkness overwhelmed her. She was sure that her father was up. She was also sure that he had heard her come in at the door. It was very disquieting to head up the stairs and to hear no sound of movement or life from the study. The quiet could not last. She interpreted the silence to mean that James had decided to speak to her in the morning, and that the stillness permeating the dark expanses of the expensive, tasteful, empty house was the quiet before the storm.

She was up early because of her throbbing hand. She showered clumsily and blow-dried her hair, brushing the long silken tresses back from her face to fall in a fiery tumble about her shoulders. She applied make-up heavily to the dark shadows under her eyes in an attempt to cover them up, but she only succeeded in making her face look caked up. She creamed it off again, leaving her skin looking pale and drawn tightly across her cheekbones. Her eyes were huge.

Dressed in slim-fitting jeans and another sleeveless shirt, she ran lightly down the stairs and made for the dining-room quickly. There was no evidence of hesitation in her manner, and no sign of fear, although fear was indeed present as it prowled behind in her tracks like a beast, its rank air drying her throat and making her swallow. She almost sagged in a visible show of relief at the sight of the empty chairs pushed tidily around the mahogany table. James was not yet down. She pushed the bell that was discreetly hidden near the head chair and sat down at the table, picking up the Sunday paper that was lying at one end. Soon Elizabeth, the housekeeper and cook, appeared in the doorway, her vast bulk taking up most of the room.

'Were you wanting breakfast this morning?' she asked expressionlessly, her little pig-like eyes darting to and fro busily.

She didn't look up as she turned the page leisurely, scanning fashions ads. 'No,' she replied after a moment coolly, 'just coffee, please, and some dry toast.'

'Very well, it'll be just a minute then.' Shooting another gleaming glance at the façade of classified ads that greeted her curious stare, Elizabeth shuffled down the hall to prepare a tray.

Presently she shuffled back with the steaming coffee and toast, which was covered with a tight-fitting lid, and Katherine lowered her paper to stare into the housekeeper's colourless eyes.

'I am not free this morning for any visitors or calls, Elizabeth,' she told the heavy woman calmly. 'I will not be near the door and will not answer it at all. Tell anyone who comes that I am not at home, do you understand?'

'Yes, miss.' The housekeeper's eyes were almost sparkling; Katherine could see the tumblers in her mind ticking over in an excited way. She had no doubt that everyone in the house that morning would be informed of just who came to the Farlough residence that morning, and who had been turned away. She knew that eventually not only Joss would know, but her father also, for what Joss knew, he invariably told James. Joss was no better than a well-paid spy.

Now that she was alone, she set aside the newspaper, not bothering to make the pretence of reading without an audience. She drank her coffee and nibbled at her toast without enthusiasm. After draining the little silver pot, she rang for more, determined not to run away from the breakfast table just to avoid the confrontation with James. It was a point of honour, but she could not avoid a sigh of relief as she left the house to go out into the sunshine after a token period of waiting.

She had thought over everything as she had tossed and turned the night before. Every move on this thankless Sunday morning was as deliberate as the night before. She was not going to see Luke Dalton privately ever again. It was the only solution as far as she could see. She would continue this fight with her father alone, just as she had started it, and take the consequences as they came. It was best this way, she decided broodingly as she wandered in the general direction of the stables, contemplating the well-tended grass over which her feet moved. She washed her hands of the whole mess surrounding Luke. James would have to find another pretty pawn.

She spent a great deal of time thinking of her unknown mother, and wondering if she had been as calculating as James or merely an unsuspecting fool caught in a snare by a charming smile. She rather suspected the latter. James wouldn't have picked anything else. Katherine pitied her mother's pale, worn ghost. She also pitied herself.

The future loomed ahead like an ugly black beast. She could not see the next day, the next hour, or any brightness in the existing moment. She could not imagine what form of revenge or punishment her father was going to mete out. Without a doubt it would be cleverly calculated to bring her pain. She had rejected the idea of leaving home for the time being, and had decided to wait and see what time brought. Her bank account was generous enough for shopping luxuries, but she realised that it could not sustain actual living expenses for long. At present, there seemed nothing for her to do.

James might go as far as to kick her out of his house,

but somehow, he doubted this. He got his kicks from
trying to control the world around him, and he would
never willingly give up power over another human
being. He liked having Katherine. She was quite
certain that he had liked showering her with presents
and watching her innocent face light up with pleasure.
She was also sure that he liked to be in a position in
her life where he could do the most damage. He could
hurt her as he pleased, when she lived under his own
roof. He could dispense approval or disapproval like
God. That he was fully aware of how frustratingly
helpless she was beginning to feel, she had not a
doubt. He would know better than anyone that she
could not feasibly support herself. This was power
over her, and he loved it.

As she thought of these things, an overwhelming
sense of loneliness hit her harder than it ever had
before. The longing to talk over her problems with a
sympathetic and caring listener had her turning back
to the house to meet Luke that morning. Then she
started thinking of his possible motives for engineering
such a talk, and her low self-esteem and inability to see
herself as a person of real worth or desirability had
made her steps falter and eventually stop. But she
continued on to the stables once again. Admittedly,
Luke had not tried to manipulate her last night, but
she had trouble crediting anyone with selfless motives.
She could not see anyone wishing to befriend her
solely for herself, since all her acquaintances had been
scrutinised and established by James. Luke wanted
something from her, therefore he wanted something
from her father. Possibly, she mused, he wanted me to
keep an active eye on James and report to him any plot
or plan for his demise.

She entered the stable through the dry, airy
doorway and blessed the cool shadows and draught of

air which blew against her face. Inhaling the smells of horse, leather and hay, she walked past several full stalls without a pause and stopped in front of a wide and roomy box. A welcoming nicker came from within, and a grey muzzle was thrust over the door, the nostrils quivering enquiringly. She patted the little nose and opened the door to slip inside. There she spent some time combing the old pony's rough mane and brushing down its sides. Taking a great deal of care over each detail, she murmured and talked nonsense to a very dear friend. Misty had been her first pony, given to her when she was five years old, and though he was well past the age of any usefulness, she still spent a large amount of time with him. He made her feel a strange and sad bitter-sweet nostalgia. He made her remember squeals of delight and bouncing rides in a hazy memory of sunlight and laughter. It was an old, faded memory of innocence and happiness, of unawareness and no complications. Together, she and the old pony would walk outdoors under swaying green trees. She would sit down under a shady tree and he would stand nearby, tail twitching and nose trembling as he dreamed about his past and about dimly remembered gallops in a long ago summer-time. Katherine did not waste time thinking about lost dreams and illusions. She was too practical for that. Dreaming would not bring back the past, she always told herself. However, she did treat the pony with a considerable amount of tenderness that somehow soothed her mind and made a liar of her.

Letting the pony out into a small paddock, she walked to the shade of a large oak tree and settled under it. Now it was a waiting game. It could not be much before eleven o'clock. She was glad that she was out of sight of the house. It helped her take her mind off the immediate future. She leaned her head back against the tree and closed her eyes.

Some time later, much later, some sixth sense made her open them again. Looking up, she endeavoured to hide her apprehension at the sight of a tall, immaculate figure standing motionless in front of her. James looked very big from this position, and it didn't help her calm to feel so small and unimportant. He watched her expressionlessly as she swiftly rose to her feet. No sooner had she stood up than his open hand cracked hard across her cheekbone in a heavy blow. Taken by surprise, her head snapped back and her body was thrown against the tree. Grasping hold of the rough bark with one trembling hand, she stood with her head bent to hide behind the heavy fall of hair shielding her from his eyes. The blow on her face had numbed that side, and she cupped it with one bandaged hand. There was no feeling left in her mind; it was too numb.

'Dalton was here,' James told her conversationally, his eyes never leaving her shaking figure. 'He asked to see you and was turned away by the servants. I thought you might like to know that, but then you aren't surprised, are you? I warned you, pet. Never say I didn't. Will you see him again?'

She forced a reply through trembling lips. 'No.'

She was still looking down, with her hair falling over her face and so was unprepared for a second, heavier blow on the other side of her head. Falling down on one knee, she didn't try to get up again but instead covered her head with both arms. She didn't think and she didn't try to act. She couldn't get away from him until he was through with her. She just shut down her mind, like a piece of machinery, and tried to survive.

'You will, pet,' said James dispassionately. And with that, he turned and walked away, the sound of his footsteps rapidly fading, in the cushioning grass, to silence.

When she was sure that her father was well away from her, she rose up and shoved her hair off her face. It fell into a chaotic tumble down her back, framing a dead-looking face streaked with wetness. She reached blindly for the tree beside her and, by leaning heavily on it, managed to pull herself up to a standing position again, scrubbing at her cheeks furiously in an attempt to clear her vision. She was trying desperately to keep a tight grip of control over herself, but when a small grey nose thrust gently against her chest, she clasped the pony's head to her, bent her face to hide it in the rough, fragrant mane and sobbed as if her heart would break.

Not far away, just beside the corner of the stables, a man with the wind in his grey hair and coldness in his cruel eyes watched the young girl hug a fat, useless old pony as if she were clinging to her very last friend and his gaze was contemplative, calculating.

She somehow managed to make it to her room without being seen by the servants. She threw herself on her bed after locking her bedroom door and, exhausted from the lack of sleep the night before and still feeling deadened from shock, she not so amazingly fell asleep.

The afternoon was gone by the time she opened her eyes. She stood carefully and the room stayed where it should, so she made for the bathroom with more confidence. As she looked into her mirror, she was truly shocked at the sight. Her face had a greyish tinge to it except where the skin was puffy and pink around the sensitive eye area. There were deep circles beneath her eyes and a haunted look in their green depths. A purple darkness was already becoming apparent on the ridge of her cheekbone, and there was some slight swelling. James had hit her hard. She saw no beauty in the sight and turned away in rejection of the despairing message of that reflection. Sitting on the edge of the bath, she tried to get herself to think, to force herself through the seemingly impenetrable cottonwool-like fog of her mind, but the only thing that kept running through it over and over again was, insanely, a nursery rhyme from óne of her long since discarded children's books: *Rain, rain, go away, come back here another day*.

Was she mad? she asked herself tiredly. Was there really nothing more to expect from this life than pain, and boredom, and loneliness? Should she always be looking over her shoulder furtively and fearfully? If this was what life was all about, then she didn't want to keep on living. She was tired. She was so very tired.

After a long time, she persuaded herself that she should move to somewhere other than the hard edge of the bath, so she crept back into her bedroom and curled up on the bed. She didn't know what to do. She didn't seem to have any energy at all: even lifting her head to support it on her aching neck seemed to be too much of an effort.

The present was too much to take, let alone any consideration of the future. An intolerable burden sat about her, stifling her with its weight and oppression. For a long time, she lay on her bed in the semi-darkness, a lonely figure afraid to face the storm.

CHAPTER FOUR

'MISS FARLOUGH? Miss Farlough?' A knock on her bedroom door and Elizabeth's voice calling, roused her from her lethargy.

'What is it?'

'You have a telephone call. Are you going to receive it?'

She sighed, slipping off her rumpled bed and flicking on a light. Moving over to her mirror, she quickly brushed her hair from her forehead with a few flicks of her brush and said expressionlessly, 'Yes. I'll be right there.'

She went downstairs quickly and picked up the phone. 'Katherine Farlough,' was her brief and crisp enunciation.

'Why wouldn't you see me this morning, Kate?' She had never heard him on the phone before, but she immediately recognised Luke's deep, controlled voice. The sound of it had her clasping the receiver in a tight clench as she pressed it painfully to her sore head.

'It wouldn't have done any good,' she replied coolly. 'You must excuse me. I'm very——'

'Don't hang up!' he cut through her swiftly muttered excuses. 'I still would like to talk to you. Can we get together, perhaps tomorrow?'

'No.'

'Please.' His voice was as quiet as hers.

'No.'

'Why are you doing this?' he asked, in a puzzled tone. 'You know you aren't happy, you know your father is trying to rule your life to the extent that he is ruining you! For the love of all that's good, why won't you let me help you?' The concern in his voice was her undoing.

Katherine closed her eyes. A sneaky tear slipped down her cheek, and another followed, and then another. 'I can't,' she whispered brokenly, catching her breath in furious reaction to her own loss of control. 'I—oh, you don't understand! I just can't!'

'No,' he agreed gently, 'I don't understand. I don't understand what has made your father the way he is. I don't understand why you feel that now, of all times, you must defy him past the point of reason. I don't understand why you won't talk to me, let me help you. Kate, let me come over tomorrow and see you. Please let me come.'

'You don't understand me, well, I don't understand you!' She tried to keep her voice down, but in spite of herself her tone rose and made it quite obvious to him just how upset she really as. It wobbled horribly. 'You are a stranger! I don't know you, why should I trust you? Why should I listen to you, of all people? Who do you think you are, anyway? What do you want from me?'

There was a silence from the other end. 'This is probably very hard for you to believe,' he said softly, 'but, I don't want a thing from you.' She was silent, breathing hard and holding on to the phone as if it were a lifeline. 'I do, however, want a great deal *for* you. But you've been brought up in a different way. You probably don't have a clue as to what I mean, do you? Do you have a pencil?'

'Yes,' she whispered through dry lips. Her hand found and gripped a writing utensil, almost of its own volition.

'I can't do a thing for you unless you want me to. Will you take down my home phone number? Will you keep it, and if you find that things are getting to be too much, will you call me?'

'No, I can't.' She barely managed to make herself

heard, the longing to do just what he asked almost too great to resist. 'It's what my father wants me to do——'

'No, love. Can't you see? James can't do a thing to you or me, now that we know what it is he's attempting with both of us,' he told her patiently. 'He has power over you through your fear. You're so busy thinking of him as the omnipotent god, you can't see beyond his domination! It's not your father you are afraid of now. It is yourself. Kate. You make your own happiness. Everyone in this world makes their own happiness. Now, pick up that pencil, and take down this number. It's . . .' As he told her the phone number clearly, repeating it once, she found her hand moving awkwardly across the notepad and taking it down. 'Call me, Kate. Any time of the day or night is fine—three in the morning if you have to! I'll wait to hear from you, and won't phone again, because now it's up to you. No one can do it for you.' He paused as if waiting for her to respond and when she didn't, he sighed and said, 'I hope to talk to you later. Goodbye for now.'

'Luke?' she said clearly, still clutching the phone tightly.

'Yes?'

She paused a long time, hearing in the background the old grandfather clock that was ticking slowly, inexorably. 'Thank you.'

After she had heard him hang up, she stood for a long while with the receiver in one hand and her eyes staring unseeingly at the opposite wall. The ticking of the clock was so ominous and frightening; she found a strange fear gripping her tightly, shaking her resolve with icy fingers. After a bit, she recollected herself with a start, placed the receiver gently on its rest, and headed back up the stairs. 'Elizabeth?' she called, halting just once half-way up.

A figure at the end of the hallway appeared. 'Did you want something, Miss?'

'Yes, a supper tray to my room, if you would. I won't be down tonight. Would you please tell James for me? I have a headache. I think he'll understand.' This last she said with a great deal of dryness.

'I'll tell him. What would you like on your tray?'

'Whatever, anything. It doesn't matter.' As she moved on up the stairs, Elizabeth retreated back to her kitchen and food, shaking her head in ponderous exasperation.

Katherine paced the length of her room, mulling over Luke's words. How could she have been so blind? It was true, James's plan would've worked only if he had her co-operation and Luke's ignorance. She had thoroughly scotched his chances for getting Luke off his guard. She had let her own fear create an obstacle where one did not exist. It had to be admitted that he would try to think of some other way either of publicly humiliating Luke or financially ruining him, but he would find another way without her, and she wouldn't be able to stop him.

What had angered James so much, she was beginning to see, was not that his little ploy to cast her after Luke had failed, but that it was she who had defied him and had caused it to fail. She was just understanding that her defiance and obstinacy was what had made him strike out at her. Probably he was already plotting some other sordid business scheme for Luke to crash into, and had put her rebellion down as an annoyance, and a temporary one at that.

How belittling it all was! She now saw that James had been right to consider her little storm in a teacup a minor and trifling thing. He had her past performance to base his opinion on. His domination of her whole life was her own fault. She had practically given herself to him on a silver platter when she had attended all those social functions at his insistence. She had sold her own soul to him very cheaply when she had gone out with the businessmen of his choice. She had bartered her self-respect for an escape from freedom. Katherine had a sneaking suspicion that she had been trying to make her father show some sign of approval, some sign of encouragement. She wanted to make him care.

Luke had been right: she was afraid of herself and of stepping out. Freedom was a heavy and frightening gift for one who had known nothing but the indolence of domination. Freedom for Katherine meant having to pay her own bills, and make her own decisions and face numerous responsibilities. If she stepped out, she would never have the excuse, 'It's not my fault! I didn't mean to do it! He made me!'

A tray was brought to her room, with the message that her father wished to speak to her in the morning, but Katherine, wrapped up in her own thoughts, dismissed this ominous-sounding message with no more than an absent-minded—and wholly un-quaking—nod. She put her tray on a little dresser beside her bed and climbed in. After uncovering one plate and picking up a delicate sandwich to nibble, she suddenly looked up and around her, as if seeing her room for the first time in her life.

A goose-down quilt graced the spacious bed, and there were several hundred dollars-worth of cosmetics on the elegant antique dressing table. Heavy oak dressers, a matching pair, stood as sentinels at either side of the roomy bedroom, and a walk-in wardrobe held expensive, glittering, fashionable clothes. Her bathroom was spacious also, with a double bath of marble, and antique brass water controls. A carelessly tossed silk dressing-gown lay in a crumpled heap by the bath, and heavy plush towels were folded precisely, awaiting her use. The mirror was framed in gilt. Several different exclusive perfumes and bath oils were scattered about haphazardly, the tops pushed on anyhow, with no respect for their famous labels.

The sandwich, she noticed, as she suddenly looked down at what she held in her hand, was crabmeat salad, tasty, tempting, and delicious. It was also very expensive.

Katherine put down her half-eaten sandwich slowly. The pretty bird preferred captivity to the dangers of the wild, did she? She could not support herself in such a style if she were to leave home. Was she indeed selling herself, for the price of her own self-respect and a paltry few blows about the head, for a life such as this? Did all the material things that money could buy really mean so much to her? Was she so afraid that she might fail utterly and humiliatingly if she were to leave, and was that keeping her here? Was this, in spite of all her protestations to the contrary, where she wanted to be?

She moved to the mirror slowly, as if compelled by some inner force greater than herself, and looked into it. What she saw was not some darling of Kentucky's high society, nor did she see the spoiled bitch who made cocktail parties so much fun. She did not see one of the most beautiful young women ever to have graced the backs of the spirited thoroughbreds that made the Blue Grass state famous. She did not see a romantically spirited young girl who had stood before an ogre of a father and dramatically defied him to the very gates of hell. She saw a very sad and rather frightened little girl with shadows under her eyes and a dull, unnecessary bruise on her cheek.

It was enough. She stared at herself for a long, long time and took a good look at the person without the pretence. She didn't want to forget the sight. She wanted to remember every single aspect that made this person who she was. She wanted to remember, so that she would not make the same mistakes again. She would never be what this person was, not ever again. Then, going to the walk-in wardrobe and dragging out, not the expensive Italian leather suitcases she'd bought for one of her recent trips, but two canvas tote bags that had seen better days, she dumped them by the bed and started to pull out various items of clothing, throwing them on the bed by the half-eaten sandwich.

After she had a pile of lacy underwear and nightgowns, dressing-gowns and tights, she rummaged about for summer shirts and shorts, digging out several pairs of jeans and sandals, and a few skirts and dresses. Then, tossing it all together in an unceremonious heap, she looked from the pile of clothing to the two small canvas bags and began to sort out what was not absolutely necessary on to the floor on the other side of the bed. She found herself at war with what her practical mind told her was necessary, and what her inner self whispered to her to take. She limited herself strictly to one pair of flat sandals, one pair of tennis shoes, one pair of casual shoes—which she set aside for wearing tomorrow—and one pair of high-heeled shoes. Then she threw aside the high-heeled shoes as not necessary after all. She would not part with one item of lacy underwear—they took up so little room, after all!—and these were quickly packed. She sat back on her heels and held up several pair of cobweb-delicate tights. They would be full of runs soon enough. She stuffed them into the canvas bag that held her underwear.

After much deliberation, she finally ended up with

two skirts, two dresses and two pairs of jeans, with a cunning asortment of tops that would be interchangeable with all. Two items she laid out: a pair of jeans and a pretty ruffled shirt to be worn tomorrow. The rest she put into a bag. Happily, after finding that she had a little room to spare after the removal of the clothes she was to wear tomorrow, she picked up the discarded high-heeled sandals and tucked them into the bag with a shimmery gold dress.

She set the two packed bags by the door and went to rummage through her purse, adding to it only one spray of French perfume, a toothbrush and some essential items of make-up. Then, satisfied with her evening's work, she sat down to munch heartily on the sadly crushed sandwich and the remainder of her meal. It was late when she finished, so she didn't attempt to phone Luke.

After crawling into bed in the summer's darkness, she lay curled up under the goose-down quilt, aquiver with excitement, anticipation and dread. Miss Farlough, for the first time in many years, was most certainly not bored. She was positively scared stiff. She didn't sleep a wink all night. She felt as if her stomach was going to give up all her dinner. She wanted to cry and, crazily, she wanted to laugh.

The pretty bird was about to fly her cage.

When the grey tendrils of light wafted away the darkness, and yet before one could precisely call it dawn, she threw back her covers and gladly got up. She showered quickly, not even sending the multitude of fragrant bath oils one regretful glance, and dried her hair. Then she slipped into her jeans and clumsily put on her shoes. A light cream-coloured blouse went on next, and then, because it was a favourite of hers and if she wore it that meant she could take it with her, she also slipped on a white angora sweater. Then, with a quick glance at the clock, she stealthily slipped out of her room and lightly skipped down the stairs. Five-thirty was a bit too early for just about anyone in the household, even for her father, for though he worked extremely hard at his business, he still kept banker's hours. Not even the omnipresent Joss would be up, she knew, especially since her own hour for rising was usually around eight. This all is, she thought, probably out of character for me, and she had to stifle what sounded horrifyingly like a giggle. She had a nasty suspicion that from now on, she was going to be doing things that a lot of people would term 'out of character' for her.

It wasn't, she reflected more soberly, as if she had possessed much character to begin with. In fact, hindsight showed her that she must have acted for several years with a remarkable *lack* of sincere character. The library door was ajar, so she decided to use the phone in there and close the door behind her, just in case.

This is stupid, she told herself severely, as her hand began to shake when she picked up the telephone receiver. She pulled out the number that she had hastily shoved in the pocket of her jeans and dialled, not giving herself time to think and perhaps back out. As she listened to the phone ring, she was aware of the most terrific feeling of panic she had ever experienced, and when a deep, alert yet quiet voice answered, she nearly put down the phone to run away.

'Hello? Hello? Who is this?' It was, of course, Luke, and he was becoming very impatient.

'I am trying,' she said as matter-of-factly as possible, 'not to hang up on you.'

'Katherine,' he breathed, incredibly sounding happy. Then, in quite a different tone of voice, far more matter-of-fact than she had been able to achieve, he replied, 'Well, I'm very glad that you didn't, because I would have taken you for a crank caller, and five-thirty is a very rude time to be making crank phone calls.'

'I'm sorry,' she said instantly. 'I know I shouldn't have rung so early. You go back to bed, and I'll phone back a little later, all right?'

'No, it's not all right, because I wasn't in bed, and you're trying to back out of whatever you wanted to say to me,' he retorted swiftly. 'Out with it, love.'

'You actually were up at this hour of the morning?' she asked, astounded. 'I've never known anyone to do that before. The only reason why I'm up so early is because I couldn't sleep and nobody else is up at this time of the morning around here.'

'I am,' he told her patiently, 'a morning person, and quit prevaricating. Were you calling to invite me over to have that talk this morning? You can do no less, since you did promise me, you know.'

'Actually——' she whispered, afraid. She was afraid of him, of herself, and very much afraid that she was about to make the biggest mistake of her life. 'I, uh, would like to take you up on that offer you made on Saturday night about . . .' Her voice petered out. She couldn't go on if her life depended on it.

'. . . about staying with me for a while until you figure out what to do?' he finished for her. 'I had Marian, my housekeeper, air a bedroom and put sheets on the bed after I spoke to you.' His voice was so comfortingly placid that she found a measure of calm returning to her. 'I had hoped, you see, that you would be calling me back fairly soon, although I never dreamed that it would be this quick. When can I come and pick you up? Will it take you long to pack?'

'I packed last night,' she told him brightly, and then her voice broke. 'I had to, you know. Things did get to be too much. You were so right, yesterday. I went up to my room and thought all evening about it and I—I, well, I just have to get out of here!' She stopped altogether and stood blinking rapidly to make the tears go away, appalled at how easily she was losing her composure lately.

'I know. I know. It's all right, Katie dear. I do understand,' his voice was very calm and extremely soothing, and he spoke in a monotone which made her breathe easier and unclench her fist without really knowing how it happened. 'I'll be there as soon as I can. I have to wake Jana—she's my sister—and let her know what is going on, and it will take me about, say, twenty minutes to drive over. Can you manage until then?'

'Oh, yes,' she assured him quickly. 'I think I'll—write my father a note, just to let him know what I've done. Do you think it's very cowardly of me, to just write a note?'

'Not if that's what you want to do,' he told her. 'If you think it would help to see him and talk to him, and yet you're too apprehensive to meet him alone, I will be more than happy to see him with you. In fact,' he continued grimly, 'it might be for the best, since I can think of a few choice things to say to Farlough, myself.'

'No,' she demurred quickly. 'I think we can forgo that encounter. I'll stick to the note and stay out of the way until you get here, for he is an early riser although this is a bit too early still. Maybe I'll go down to the stables, and contrive to disappear until you come.'

'That might be the best idea,' he agreed, albeit a little reluctantly. 'I'll see you in about half an hour, then. Kate, I'm glad you did decide to call me. You won't regret it.'

'You must be joking,' she told him succinctly. 'I

already am regretting it, as well you should know. See you.'

She decided to stay away from the stables after all. It would only bring her heartache, for the little pony, Misty, wouldn't know any better. He was the only horse that she was attached to. The others were showy, high-spirited animals, good for a tearing gallop across the fields but too bad tempered and spoiled to be held in any deep affection. A quick trip to the kitchen had her carrying back to her father's study a steaming cup of coffee, instant, but better than waiting for a percolated cup she wouldn't have time to drink.

In her father's large study she headed for the covered typewriter at a desk that his personal secretary used from time to time, and plugged it in. Setting the steaming mug down close by, she was soon embroiled in a difficult letter in which she attempted to convey a sense of independence without rebellion, a detachment without resentment, and a clear refusal to be manipulated without fear. She failed, dismally. As she tore the sheet out of the humming typewriter in disgust and ripped it to pieces, two things happened. She heard quite clearly the sound of firm footsteps on the staircase just outside the study door and went into a panic. However, a knock then sounded at the front door quietly, which had the same effect on her as the signal of a hero rescuing a damsel from a dragon's ire.

She jumped up and turned off the typewriter, while one cool part of her whispered that she was very definitely acting out of character—she'd never acted this foolishly in her life. After rushing to the study door and about to hurry into the hall, something, some quietly whispered word of caution from the same part of her brain, had her stopping just inside the doorway and barely out of sight of the front door. She could hear perfectly the measured footsteps as they continued down the stairs to head, she knew, for the door. A lock was turned, and the door opened wide, and James spoke very civilly, with only a hint of well-bred surprise, 'Good gracious, Luke! This is a bit unusual for a social call, don't you think? Do step in, man, step in! What brings you here, ah, so bright and early?'

A casually amused voice answered him, deep and immensely welcome to her ears. 'I might ask you just about the same thing, James, but instead of asking "What are you doing *here!*" I would ask you "What are you doing *up?*" Is Katherine around?'

'She's not exactly in the habit of rising so early,' her father replied, ostensibly still in the same polite tone but with an underlying hint of anger becoming apparent. 'What did you need?'

'Your daughter,' said Luke easily. 'I've come to fetch her.'

'You've what?' There were the tiny beginnings of satisfaction in James's voice; Katherine could tell just what he was thinking. He thought she had planned some outing with Luke after her encounter with him yesterday.

'I said I've come to fetch her. She's leaving home, didn't she say?' Under his light and easy tone, she thought—she wasn't sure, but she thought—she could detect a certain thread of hardness in his voice. It was very slight, and much more subtle than James's own note of anger, but it had her thanking providence that she was not on the receiving end of that speech. 'But perhaps she didn't. Things, I understand, have been a bit . . . shall we say, unsettled around here? I daresay she forgot.'

'Just what in hell do you mean "she's leaving home" and "she forgot to say"?' James demanded harshly. She stiffened.

'I should think,' replied Luke, 'that it is fairly clear. Is she around?'

'You aren't going to see her this early in the morning,' James stated coldly and precisely. 'Now, get out, and come back later, when the household is up and so is Katherine, and we'll straighten out just exactly what is going on!'

'My!' exclaimed Luke with interest. 'You've certainly changed your tune, Farlough. I thought you wanted nothing more than for me to welcome your beautiful and desirable daughter into my eager arms! Have you changed your mind, perhaps set up a better thought-out plan of action for my demise? Let me know, will you? And I would like to add that I'd prefer to talk to Katherine before you've had a chance to see her in private and maybe change her mind.'

'I think,' commented James calmly, after a moment, 'that I'm going to kill her for that.'

'I think,' replied Luke gently, and every bit as calmly as he, 'not.'

At this, she burst out of the shadowed doorway where she had been lurking and she hurried to the front door in no small state of agitation. Luke was leaning against the doorpost in a position of indolent laziness, his black hair blown about his lean, hard face. He had on a faded pair of jeans, a dark blue roll-neck sweater, and an easy smile, but when she looked up into his dark eyes, she was considerably taken aback at the sight of a dark flame of rage kindled and burning deep within. His arms were folded across his wide chest, and one casually shod foot was kicked across the other.

James, dressed casually for him, was considerably more elegant in expensive slacks and a smoking jacket over a cream sweater. His light hair was brushed immaculately back off his forehead. He also was in a towering rage, she saw, as she stared into those cold, cold eyes. She got the strangest feeling when she looked into James's eyes. To look into total emptiness ... She had never realised just how destructive her father's comprehension of life really was, and she grasped his amorality for a brief, chilling moment as she stared into a pit devoid of human compassion or understanding. She gasped in shock. She was looking into the pitiless eyes of a serpent.

'Ready, love?' A deep, chocolatey rich voice broke the spell of James's viciousness and she turned, considerably startled, to face warm grey eyes, intelligent, amused, caring. As she turned to face Luke fully, though, the look vanished to be replaced with such an expression of fury that she involuntarily took a step back. It was unlike anything she had seen.

He launched away from the doorpost and swiftly reached her side, taking her chin with gentle fingers, his face masked after that one instant of naked anger. That incredible fury still lurked in his eyes, she found, though, as she looked up. 'Who hit you in the face, my dear?' he asked calmly.

Katherine, hating every minute of the unpleasant scene, was shaking rather violently and he must have been able to feel it, for his cool fingers tightened fractionally on her chin. However, a lifetime of acting and a certain amount of pride made her answer very coolly, 'It doesn't matter. Truly. Quite unimportant, Luke, I really mean it, but don't you think we should be going?'

After studying her for an instant, he answered reflectively, 'Yes, I suppose we must. Where are your bags?'

'Katherine, you aren't going anywhere,' James stated calmly, and yet with an underlying threat that had her blinking and considering that perhaps she shouldn't go after all. Her eyes reflected their uncertainty. 'Dalton, get away from my daughter and get out. Don't make me use force! This farce has gone on long enough.' He stepped forward and stopped as Luke whirled, a threat implicit in his body movement. The two men faced each other, the older man bulkier and certainly taller, and powerful in spite of his additional years. Katherine took several steps back as she looked apprehensively from one man to the other. Luke, after his swift turn about, stood easily with hands on hips and feet a little apart. He appeared relaxed even though he stood on the balls of his feet, ready for any event. In his eyes it was possible to see a touch of anticipation and—was it by any chance eagerness? Looking from one to the other, she couldn't say why, but Katherine began to relax. She would lay odds on Luke, any day.

'Get your bags, Katie,' said Luke pleasantly, without looking about. 'I'll, er, keep James company down here.'

Taking another peep at her father's by now thunderous face, she spun on her heel, and fled.

Careering out on to the landing with her bags and scrambling down the stairs, she was vaguely surprised—and secretly disappointed—to see both men still standing, in fact in the same positions that they had occupied when she had so hastily left. She stopped, heaving a bit, just behind Luke's shoulder, and was immediately struck by the fact that she had done so very naturally.

'All set?' asked Luke lightly, not looking around. She uttered an affirmative, and he continued, 'Well, I'll say this for you, sweetheart, you're quick. Go and get into the car like a good girl. I'll be there in a moment.'

'Oh, but I'd rather——' began Katherine, and was cut short by one quietly spoken word.

'Go,' he said, and she took a hesitant look around his broad shoulder at the murderous look on James's face. She inched for the door.

'I suppose that you won't be needing anything else but what you have, darling?' James said suddenly, causing her to look at him in puzzlement. 'I can get rid of anything else?' His eyes watched her cruelly, mockingly. 'After all, your possessions mean nothing to me . . .' What was his threat? she asked herself, frightened. I can't figure out his threat. '. . . and, of course, Misty is too old to be of any use to anyone, isn't he?'

Her face blanched and after a minute, she closed her eyes, sickened. James watched her tortured face, and he smiled. Unaware of anything outside her own pain, not even aware of Luke, she turned again to the door and started to walk stiffly towards it, her head bent and her eyes blurred. Each step was a death sentence to a little pony who deserved nothing less than a peaceful retirement under the shade of an apple tree, and lazy afternoons filled with wordless dreams.

'So, when you leave . . .' James continued, and she forced herself on, '. . . I'll just make a—clean sweep, so to speak.' She opened the door and hesitated. She very nearly couldn't stand it. She very nearly gave in and turned back. 'Misty shouldn't feel much. I should think it would be just a twinge, when the vet gives him his shot . . .' She teetered on the brink of surrender, and stepped back. James would only inflict more pain on her, and Misty had lived a good life. With a great effort, she stepped out of her father's house, across the threshold. She shut the door gently behind her and slowly, dully, climbed into Luke's car after depositing her bags in the back. She waited.

After a few minutes, Luke came out and he slid into the sports car. He looked at her searchingly, and after a quick glance at him that revealed hair a bit more ruffled than before and the knuckles on his big right hand reddened, she turned and stared straight ahead silently. 'All right?' he asked carefully, starting the car and easing into the drive.

'Perfect,' she stated, and promptly burst into tears.

He let her cry without interference, and only occasionally shot her searching and concerned glances. They made the drive to his house in near silence. After a bit, she was able to contain herself to just a few odd tears that slid down her face from time to time as she dully looked out of the window at the passing grey world.

When he pulled into a large driveway that formed a huge sweep in front of a charming brick colonial house, she was able to look about her with a semblance of interest. He swung round and parked in front of the white-painted doors and turned to her with a wry smile.

'I left Jana in a pleasant dither,' he told her, amused. 'She told me to bring you straight home, and not even attempt to offer you breakfast out since she had every intention of fixing you something here! I hope you like her, Kate,' he continued a bit diffidently for him, 'she so loves company and she gets so little that she's likely to smother you with attention! She is, I believe, eccentric.'

This easy talk had her looking at him, first with a deal of genuine interest and later with some amusement. 'She sounds like a character,' Katherine said, delighted. 'Why do you say that she's eccentric?'

'Well, she loves lame ducks and stray dogs and lost kittens,' he replied, grinning. 'We usually have no fewer than a half a dozen grouped around our back porch with hopeful expressions on their various furry faces! She also runs around in either wild caftans or ominous black, depending on the impression she wishes to portray. It will be interesting to see what she is wearing this morning in honour of your arrival! She has the most lovely black hair with touches of grey at the temples that she laments at any opportunity, and very blue eyes that twinkle at the slightest provocation! She is apt to play either loud rock music or impressive classical at earth-shaking volumes and at very shocking times of the day! In short, my dear, Jana is extremely happy and always herself, no matter who that might be at the time!'

'Oh dear,' she murmured faintly. 'I do so hope that she doesn't choose black for this morning! I'm quite sure that I would be deflated at that message! Do you think she will dislike me? That would be terribly awkward.'

'Of course she won't,' he assured her with a wide grin which displayed his even, white teeth. 'She always likes the people that I do.'

She was at a loss as to how to reply to this and finally murmured, 'Thank you. Is my face very smudged?' This last was asked anxiously. 'I feel like I have gritty sand in my eyes; they burn quite painfully.'

He studied the pale and tired face speculatively. 'I expect it is because you haven't had very much sleep and then topped it off by crying,' he said. 'Your eyes do look a bit red, and you look very tired, and of course that bruise doesn't help matters very much. In fact, you look a bit like a little stray cat that I picked up off the streets. No, I daresay that Jana will fall in love with you at once, and stop rubbing that eye, you're only making it worse! You know,' he added reflectively, 'I can't figure out how it is that you can look at once so very haggard, and yet at the same time quite beautiful too. I suspect that it is the effect of those incredible eyes!' He smiled at her so sweetly that she forgot her burning eyes and her general misery enough to smile back, as sweetly, to him. 'Come on!' he commanded, suddenly brisk. 'Let's go and see what crazy caftan Jana's got on today!'

And with that, they both climbed out of the car, Luke doing so quickly and Katherine more hesitantly. He came round the car to put one reassuring arm about her shoulder as he led her up the wide steps and across the spacious porch to the door. He opened it and ushered her in without ceremony, closing the door behind and calling out, 'Jana! Jana, you abominable sister, where are you? I've brought Kate here!'

A small head poked from a doorway down the hall. 'You needn't roar,' the stern admonishment was administered with an amused light voice. A delicately boned and slim body followed the little head and Katherine stared into lovely blue eyes that danced up at her. 'And this is Katherine!' the small woman exclaimed with every sign of satisfaction. She ran a swift and careless hand through a cloud of lovely long dark hair, streaked with grey. Her eyes suddenly sharpened at the sight of Katherine's bruise, and she sent a very piercing look at Luke as she scolded him lightly for taking much longer than he had promised. She received a negative shake of the head from him in reply which Katherine didn't see as he was standing behind her. She continued gaily, 'I wanted so badly to put on black this morning, love, since it is so dismal and dull outside, but I thought instead that I'd put on a bit of colour for your arrival! Now, Luke, go and get her bags, and I'll show you where your room is, all right?'

Katherine smiled slightly at this and nodded. The older woman tucked her arm through hers with such a childishly confiding air that she was quite disarmed, and soon was chuckling at Jana's nonsensical and wholly good-natured teasing. They made their way to the second floor where Jana led her to the first room on the left with the door ajar.

Entering the room, Katherine was pleasantly surprised to find a very comfortable décor. It was not a particularly large room—in fact it was much smaller than she was used to—but it was quite charming with various rugs on a polished wood floor and a huge double-poster bed, canopied and draped with a brightly printed quilt. There were two doors, one leading she found to a tiny private bathroom, and the other being the wardrobe. An antique desk stood daintily just in front of a frilly-curtained window. Jana was watching her look about with pleasure, her own kind eyes smiling, and then said with a brisk friendliness, 'I'll leave you alone for a few minutes to get acquainted with the room! I'm sure that Luke will be up in a moment with your bags—please, let me know if Marian has forgotten anything trifling, like the towels for the bathroom, or sheets for the bed. She is hopelessly forgetful ...' Still chattering laughingly, Jana floated out of the room with a quick wave of the hand.

Left to her own devices for the moment, she headed for the bathroom after a bit of inspection, and ruthlessly splashed cold water on her face in an attempt to put some colour into her cheeks.

As she turned to leave the little bathroom she found Luke propping up the doorway.

'Hello,' she said calmly. Her face was serious, but her eyes smiled just a little at him, and his own softened into a twinkle in response. 'I was beginning to wonder where you were. You move very quietly, don't you?'

'A habit,' he admitted, 'that makes Jana shriek! Are

you feeling up to coming downstairs and meeting Marian and the menagerie? At last count, I believe that there were three cats and a dog in temporary residence in the kitchen. Jana names every one of them, but I can never keep them straight. There's also coffee brewed, I think.'

'Coffee sounds nice,' she admitted politely, and gave a wry chuckle that sounded unamused. 'I'm sure that my cup of coffee is still sitting in James's study, unnoticed for the moment and quite cold! I didn't have a chance to finish it, as things turned out.'

'Well,' Luke commented mildly, 'we won't think about that now, if you'd rather not. I for one would like to put some distance between myself and that unpleasant interlude.'

He took her arm gently and walked with her to the door. Now that her mind was on the subject, she asked him a little stiltedly, 'Did you hit him? I got the impression that you had, although you didn't mention anything. I—if you'd rather not tell me,' she faltered, seeing his face with a curiously implacable expression, 'we can talk about something else . . .'

'And having you dwelling on it in silence anyway?' he replied, shaking his head. The look faded as he stared down into her eyes, and he smiled faintly. 'I think we should say just a bit about the subject, to clear the air. But after a little talk, we are both going to put the whole incident out of our minds, and think of nothing else but kittens and dogs and lunch for you, and work for me, for the rest of the day! Tonight will be soon enough to talk about other things.'

At the head of the stairs, he prompted her to sit down beside him on the first step. After a hesitation, he said abruptly, 'I did hit him—rather hard—but I waited until he tried to hit me first. I won't apologise;

he had been damnably cruel to you as you walked out of the door, and I——'

'I hope,' said Katherine deliberately, watching Luke as he sat with hands loosely laced between his knees and face turned away, 'that you at least managed to give him a black eye.' His head shot round and he stared at her with blackly snapping eyes that were beginning to show amusement. 'And I would be quite pleased if you had been able to knock him down, although I quite understand if you didn't. He is a big man, isn't he?' She met Luke's eyes with complete composure.

'As a matter of fact,' he acknowledged modestly, 'James was spilled all over the bottom of the staircase, but, well, I didn't mean to boast about it. If I might say so, it was a rather neatly thrown shot.' Green eyes met dark grey ones in perfect understanding.

'Serves him right,' she agreed. 'He *is* the one that gave me this memento, you know.' She touched her cheek. 'I'm much obliged to you. I would have never been able to hit him, myself.'

'Only too happy to be of service. I had suspected as much. The punch I threw at him afforded me a great deal of satisfaction.' He sat for some few minutes brooding over that satisfaction.

'Honestly, Luke,' a laughingly exasperated voice sounded at the bottom of the staircase and made both Katherine and the subject thus addressed look enquiringly below them. 'Marian is positively miffed at the pair of you! She's quite sure that you mean to avoid her, and I know that we won't get a decent meal out of her for days if she's in a huff! Now get down here, both of you, and come and have some breakfast before she hands in her notice!'

Luke threw back his head and laughed heartily at this, and Katherine's face lightened also. After watching the two stand up and start down the stairs again, Jana headed back to the kitchen with a swish of her brilliant skirts, while a smile teased her lips.

The roomy kitchen was as warm with various wriggling bodies below the knee, and alight with a hospitable glow. The deliciously tantalising smell of hot coffee pervaded the air, along with the sizzling sound of bacon frying fragrantly and toasting bread. Katherine was assailed with sharp yaps from a frantic pup that managed to get tangled up between her ankles and the pangs of hunger. She stumbled over the eager little body and, in an attempt to avoid a huge calico monster of a cat, pitched forward in what was an unavoidable fall. Two swift hands reached out from behind and grabbed her, yanking her upright.

'Okay?' he asked easily, before he relinquished his hold on her shoulders. She nodded, watching the antics of the little animals with no small degree of amusement.

Turning to glance at him with sparkling eyes, she asked, 'So, not only are you very light on your feet, you're also extremely swift! Should I, I wonder, begin to pity my father after all?'

'Hush, child,' he murmured, 'you don't know what you say.' He looked beyond Katherine, and his face lightened into a teasing expression. 'Ah, Marian, my love! I hear you're feeling sorely neglected today. Here,' and he planted a hearty kiss on a thin, wrinkled cheek, 'a peace offering, for the good of our future meals! Come meet my Katie and say you like her.' The last words put Katherine in a whirl of confusion.

Bright eyes set in a wrinkled face, under a shocking mass of red hair, met Katherine's for a long moment. She raised her eyebrows after a bit; Katherine could have sworn that she had seen mischief in those merry eyes. ' "She was the fairest creature in the world; and yet she is inferior to none".' A voice, dry like autumn leaves that are tossed in the wind and sounding every bit as merry as the eyes looked, startled Katherine considerably. Looking into her astonished face, Marian murmured, 'What an uncomfortable-looking bruise, my dear. That was *The Taming of the Shrew*, some time before the first act, in the first or second scene in the Induction, but where I haven't the foggiest.' The mischievous face turned to Luke's choking countenance. 'Don't you think it appropriate for a Kate, my dear, and a pretty one at that?'

'Oh, to be sure,' he was hasty to agree. He chuckled at the expression on Katherine's face. 'Marian,' he explained, 'is an avid reader of Shakespeare, among other things.'

'Marian,' intervened Jana sarcastically, 'is an avid reader of anything. Come and sit down, Katherine, over here. Would you like cream or sugar in your coffee?'

'Cream, please,' she murmured, feeling dazed. She allowed herself to be led to a chair.

Very soon, a steaming plate filled with bacon, toast, and eggs was set before her bemused face. To her own surprise, she managed to clear the lot. Laughing chatter accompanied the meal as Jana, Luke and even Marian sat down to breakfast also. Marian sent a wicked grin her way when she raised her eyebrows in surprise at the old woman calmly seating herself with her two employers. She said nothing, however, and merely grinned back as she forked a piece of scrambled egg into her mouth. She was content just to sit and listen to the banter that flew back and forth from one to the other. Luke teased the women unmercifully, and they laughingly retorted back. The meal was the most relaxed and amusing breakfast she had ever attended.

She was feeling exhausted at the end, and unaccountably depressed. A fresh cup of coffee sat in front of her and she stirred it automatically, as she stared into its murky depths. The weight of the future and the burden of the present was again upon her, and her shoulders bowed in dejection under the load.

'Hey,' a quiet voice broke into her thoughts. She glanced at Luke enquiringly and the sight of his lean face with the angular cheekbones and the thin hollows underneath, the firm jaw and determined lips, and those marvellous eyes struck her anew. He reached out one strong hand and clasped her two smaller ones, covering both completely and squeezing hard. She tried to smile at him, but it was a dismal failure and to her horror her eyes filled with tears. She looked away, blinking rapidly.

'It's okay to cry,' he said gently. The two women had got up and, with various muttered excuses, had left a few minutes before. Katherine tried to find within herself some semblance of pride to keep from giving in to the humiliating tears, but she found herself with a face streaked with wetness as she held her shoulder, rigid in an attempt to gain control. A chair scraped, and a strong arm came round her stiff shoulders. Giving up the battle, she turned her face into Luke's sweater and clung to his strength. Another arm slid under her knees and she was lifted on to his lap and held tightly. She was silent, determined not to make a sound and embarrass herself further by letting the two women hear her sobs, but the force of her stormy tears shook her body like a tree shuddering in the wind. After a time, she was able to relax her rigidity and curve her body more to him. An occasional tear would slide down her cheek and these were wiped away with a gentle finger by Luke.

He began to talk to her about commonplace things.

He told her that he was going to come home early and talk to her, and that she would have a nice, relaxing day to do whatever she wanted to do. 'Don't hesitate to go to bed, if that's what you want,' he told her. 'It would be understandable, considering how little sleep you've had in the past two nights. And whatever you do today, don't think about the future. Just read, or perhaps watch television, and don't feel you have to keep Jana and Marian company. I want you to feel you can take a little vacation, if you like, and not do much of anything until we all get reoriented. What do you like to read?'

She was able to answer him by then, and replied, 'I—it really depends on what you have, but I like a lot of things. A good suspense, or romance, or mystery. I usually read something light.'

He set her on her feet. 'Let's go and see what we can find, shall we?' A trip to the library found several paperback books that she declared an interest in, and Luke tucked them under his arm. 'I'll take these up to your room, so that you have them when you want them. Do you want one for now? Or did you want to do anything else today?'

She shrugged, her eyes averted. All her self-respect was gone, her pride sadly damaged. She had never cried before in front of another person, and she seemed to be crying all the time when she was with Luke.

'Well,' he said after a moment, 'I'm sure you'll find plenty to keep yourself occupied with.' There was a pause as he glanced at his wrist-watch, but she didn't notice since she was too busy not looking at him. 'Now, I'm afraid I've really got to run and change for work.' He hesitated. 'Do you think you'll be all right?'

Her head snapped up at that, like a puppet's head jerked by a string. 'Of course,' she said with dignity, almost coldly. His eyes became unreadable as he stared into her too-bright eyes, and he nodded.

'I didn't have any doubts about that,' he smiled at her quizzically. 'I'm going to run, then,' he said, and bent his head towards her a fraction. But, apparently changing his mind, he squeezed her arm gently before walking briskly out of the library. She sank into a deep armchair, feeling as if her legs had turned to noodles, and stared into space for a long time after he left.

CHAPTER FIVE

As Katherine opened the book that she was neither interested in nor that she expected to read, she let her thoughts wander where they would. She didn't have much of an opinion of herself at the moment. She didn't have much of an opinion of life, either. A heavy apathy settled over her like a dark cloak.

After a time, a sinuously graceful body slunk into the room and casually strolled towards her, tail held imperiusly high and large yellow eyes blinking. Matilda the monster leapt on to Katherine's lap and settled graciously, giving after a moment a rough-sounding purr. At this she had to smile, and she rubbed the pleased cat behind the ears. She thought sadly of her little pony, Misty, whom she couldn't help but feel she'd abandoned. She wondered if James had really held true to his threat. She didn't doubt it: he always had in the past. The pony was probably dead by now, and she felt like a murderer. What else could she have done, though? Misty had lived out a good life, whereas she was just barely starting hers. Should she have stayed, just a little while longer? Would she have survived any more of her father's cruelty?

And so was the fast morning of Katherine's liberation spent, brooding over the past and bringing up old grievances. Freedom was no different from oppression, she reflected with a bitter twist of her lips. It was all one and the same to her.

Going into the kitchen, she searched around and found a small kettle, and after filling it at the tap, she set it on a burner. She sat and waited for the water to boil, after locating some instant coffee. Soon she was heading up to her room with a steaming cup. She locked the door behind her. A strange feeling invaded her limbs, a feeling of heaviness. Her hand was throbbing painfully and irritatingly, and her eyes felt strained. After stripping off her sweater, she curled on the bed with her hot drink and sipped it lethargically. When she had finished it, she set the empty cup on the floor, stretched out on the soft, strange bed and drifted off almost immediately.

When she woke up she felt awful. A dull headache was throbbing in the back of her eyes, and she was much too hot, with a dry feeling in her mouth. She stumbled out of bed and stripped off her clothes. Then, turning on the cold water in the shower, she stepped in, gasping in shock at the stinging spray that hit her overheated back. After a few minutes she was hopping out with a shiver and drying off as fast as she could. She dressed again, wearing the same jeans but putting on a different top, and she pinned her damp hair up in a simple knot off her neck. Checking the bedside clock, she found that it was three in the afternoon, and she hurried downstairs with her empty cup dangling in one hand.

A delicious smell hit her as she entered the cosily warm kitchen. Jana was up to her elbows in flour, her hair untidily pulled back in a pony-tail that, in spite of the two grey streaks winging away at her temples, made her look absurdly young. Marian was checking something in the oven, her frizzy red hair sticking out in all directions. She was wearing a frilled apron that tied at the back. Both women looked round as the kitchen door swung open, admitting Katherine.

'Mind the animals,' warned Marian automatically, and Katherine slipped quickly through the door, letting it shut behind her.

Jana surveyed her face with approval. 'Much as I'm sorry that you missed lunch with us, I have to admit that you look a good deal better,' she said, crinkling her eyes in a friendly grin.

'I felt pretty bad when I woke up,' she said lightly, as she slipped into a chair by the table. 'I hardly ever sleep during the day. But after stepping into the ice-cold shower I had, I do feel better. I'm sorry about missing lunch.'

'Oh, don't be,' Jana reassured her. 'Never feel you have to sit down at any of our meals unless you want to. I must say, though, you missed a good meal! Marian fixed lasagne.'

'There's still some left, if you would like it reheated,' Marian offered thoughtfully, closing the door with a bang.

She declined, saying that she thought she might take a walk, if they thought it wouldn't rain. Both women looked out of the kitchen window at the dull grey sky. 'I don't think it will,' said Jana with obvious doubt.

'It doesn't matter if it does,' Marian told her. 'Just take my raincoat and go out. I do, all the time. It has a hood and will keep you quite dry.'

'I think I will,' she said. 'A walk in the rain sounds inviting.' She thanked Marian seriously, and took the raincoat off its peg, slipping it on. Going out of the back door, she told them not to expect her back at any certain time.

Outside, she took stock of her surroundings, and started towards a large clump of trees, some distance to her left. The grey day suited her mood. When a few large drops of wetness slopped on her bare head, she found the hood with one hand, reached back and put it up about her face. When she reached the trees she found a narrow footpath that she started following. It led through the thickest area of trees, into a shadowy thicket where a little of the rain reached her with big, plopping drops.

After a time she thought that maybe she should go back to the house, and she did so reluctantly, not wanting to face the kindness of the two women or Luke's homecoming. When she again opened the back door, she was thoroughly drenched, almost to her waist from the water that had dripped down the neckline of the carelessly worn raincoat. Fresh cookies were cooling on the long counter by the kitchen sink, and the smell of baking bread wafted to her flared nostrils. Marian sat at the table with a cup in front of her and a book propped in her hands. At the dripping sight of Katherine, she exclaimed and dropped the book to hurry forward.

'Why, you silly girl! Whatever possessed you to let yourself get so wet on a cold day like today?' she scolded, thrusting her hands quickly past Katherine's fumbling ones and unbuttoning the coat herself. 'Here, sit down and take out these pins! Jana, would you get a towel?' The last was yelled down the hall, and Katherine heard quick footsteps and a ready reply. 'I'm going to make you a hot drink! What do you like—do you like tea?'

'Look,' she said helplessly, her wet hair dangling thinly down her soaked back. 'This isn't really necessary, you know. I can just run upstairs and——'

'Don't give me any excuses!' Marian shushed her sternly. Her faded eyes twinkled at Katherine. 'Jana and I *like* to fuss, so don't let me hear anything more about it!'

Jana bustled in busily and shrieked at the sight of Katherine's dripping hair and streaked face. 'Here!' she exclaimed, thrusting the towel into her hands. 'Start towelling your hair dry.' Trying to dry her hair with the fluffy towel, Katherine listened to Marian's happy scoldings and to the yapping puppy that was trying to climb into her lap and to the hiss of the cats as each tumbled over the other and the dog in an effort to jump up on her. She felt quite dazed.

'Is everything always so noisy?' she asked Jana.

She laughed. 'And Marian and I thought we were having a quiet afternoon at home! No, my dear, things here are usually much worse! Here, stand up and put this round you.' She held up a heavy terrycloth dressing-gown that looked huge. Katherine stood, and Jana helped her put it on. After it was pulled round her almost twice, and belted firmly into place, Jana made her sit down again.

Thus it was that when Luke walked quietly into the kitchen with his business suit and tie still on, he saw two cats perched precariously on Katherine's lap, shedding hair all over his favourite blue terrycloth dressing-gown and Marian and Jana chatting over a cup of tea while the younger girl listened. He looked Katherine over, from the half-damp hair that was curling at her temples to the voluminous garment she was practically drowning in, and the small stockinged feet that peeped out of her darkened and damp jeans. 'Did you go walking in the rain? I like to do so, myself, on occasion.'

She brought herself to smile a little at his friendly welcome, but the smile didn't reach her eyes, and he stared at her thoughtfully for a minute, his eyes narrowed on her. Then, he said briskly, 'Do you suppose that I might be allowed a drink of something, Marian, before supper? No, not tea! Something a little more substantial, if you please. A glass of wine would be nice, thank you.' He pulled up a chair and sat for a moment exchanging pleasantries with his sister while studying Katherine. Shifting a bit under the scrutiny of his keen eyes, she pushed the two cats off her lap and stood up.

'I think I'll get some dry clothes on,' she murmured quietly and escaped upstairs to the emptiness of her room. Before she had changed she sat on her bed for a few minutes, wondering just why she had taken off in such a panic. Footsteps sounded in the corridor and went by her room without stopping. Roused by this, she took off her damp jeans and top, to replace them quickly with another pair of jeans and warm sweater. Soon footsteps were heading back for the stairs, but this time they stopped, and a knock sounded at her door.

'Yes?' she called out, without opening it.

'I have just been to my room and have changed into more casual clothes, so I know that you've had more than enough time.' Luke's voice sounded deeply through the panels. 'Quit hiding and come out to play, Katie-bug! Would you like some wine to sip? I want to hear about your day.'

She could think of no excuse to give him for staying in her room, so after a moment she opened the door to stare at him expressionlessly. His black hair had just been recently brushed, and he looked fresh in faded jeans with a black sweater, long sleeved, with the arms pulled up to his elbows showing a good amount of dark heavy hair sprinkled over tough-looking muscled forearms. He smiled at her easily, but she thought for a moment that she had glimpsed puzzlement deep in his eyes. Looking again to assure herself if that was what she saw, Katherine told herself that she must have been mistaken; there was nothing but a warm smile in those grey eyes. She handed him his dressing-room.

'Thank you for the use of your dressing-gown,' she said politely. 'I'm sorry about the cat hairs.' Her green eyes held nothing but a careful blankness.

'It's all right,' he replied, taking it and tossing it

over one arm. 'I'll go and drop it off in my room, if you want to go on down to the library.'

She ran lightly down the stairs and ensconced herself in one of the comfortable armchairs, waiting patiently and quite numbly for Luke to reappear, which he did quite soon, carrying two glasses, one half empty, of wine. He handed the full one to her, sat down in a nearby chair, and sipped his wine with appreciation. She thought as she looked at him that he certainly looked full of vitality. In fact, she was sure that she looked more haggard than he did. He watched her from under thick and level brows, and smiled. 'How did you spend your day?'

'I took a nap and took a walk,' she said. He raised his eyebrows mockingly at that.

'My! You must be as happy to sit down as I am!' She said nothing to this, merely sipping at her glass to provide an excuse for not answering his light mockery. 'How are you feeling?' The question was delicately put.

'Fine.' She refused to give anything away. It was, she thought, a matter of pride.

'Are you?' His tone was something she wasn't sure that she liked, and her head jerked up sharply. 'And,' he continued softly, 'have you figured out just what you would like to do with yourself?'

'No.' She looked away and refused to look at him again.

'Have you any idea as to what you might be interested in? Secretarial work? Something more physical? Something with people?'

'No!' With an effort she controlled her rising voice. 'I really don't know. Look, can we talk about this some other time, maybe tomorrow?' She set her wine glass down and stood up, pacing the long length of the room impatiently. Away from Luke, at the other end of the room, she stood facing the wall, with her arms wrapped around herself as if in protection. 'How was your day?' she asked after a moment, unable to stand the silence.

He didn't answer. Instead, she heard slow footsteps behind her as he came up to her and touched her shoulder gently. 'Where are you, Katie?' he asked her whimsically. 'I can't seem to find you under all that expressionlessness. Why are you hiding? What are you really feeling?'

With a suddenness that surprised them both, she broke away from his light touch, moving agitatedly away, with jerky uncontrolled movements. 'I don't know,' she blurted out, unable to stop herself. Running a rough hand through her hair and making it glint in the soft light, she whispered, 'I don't know what to feel. I don't know what to look forward to. I don't know what to think, or how to act!' Her voice rose in spite of herself, as all the feelings that she had kept in spilled out in a confused outcry. 'I'm depressed, and I don't know why! I don't like it here, I don't like it at home! I don't want to think of the future, and I can't help thinking about the past, and I'm . . . I'm——'

'—afraid,' he finished softly, and put two big hands on her shoulders as he moved up behind her once again. She started to move away, and his fingers tightened on her. 'And,' he added thoughtfully, 'you're probably confused, and most likely very bitter . . .' He drew her back and pulled her against his strong, supportive body. She found herself sagging almost automatically to his lean length, and he put his chin on her head.

She was tense and shaking very slightly. 'And angry,' she admitted, 'and sorry, and——'

His head lifted as if in surprise. 'Sorry?' he asked quickly. 'Why are you sorry?'

She sighed. 'I keep thinking about poor Misty. He didn't deserve to die, he should have had a good long retirement with nothing to do or worry about other than how many apples he could eat in an afternoon, and I—I practically murdered him by leaving like I did . . .' she choked, unable to go on for a minute. She sobbed harshly but caught herself. 'I—he was my only friend, a pony that was given to me when I was five, and it's stupid to feel so badly about a crazy horse, but—he was the only happiness that I knew at home.' Her breath was coming in jagged gasps that she tried desperately to control. 'And, he just reminded me of better times, and . . .' She was turned into his comforting arms and a hand cradled her head into his shoulders, '. . . and I wish I'd quit crying into your shirts!'

At this, his chest shook a bit, and he bent his head to bury his lips in her hair. 'It's okay,' he murmured. 'I wouldn't let just anyone, but you I kind of like.'

That had her laughing almost hysterically, and he pulled her away from him to frown into her brimming eyes. 'I know,' she gulped. 'I'm trying to stop, really.'

'Good,' he told her. Leading her back to her chair, he pushed her gently into it, and handed her the wine she'd put down. 'Finish it. It'll help a bit.' He knelt beside her chair and watched her drink it in slow sips. When she seemed calmer, he started to talk. 'Katie, you've got to stop feeling remorse. You didn't kill that horse, your father did. I'm sorry about Misty, but from the sound of things, he was an old pony. Did he have a good life?'

Unable to look up, she nodded slightly. A long finger came up and rubbed her nose, making her blink.

'Don't you think he would be better off being put to sleep, after having a good life, instead of getting so decrepit that he could hardly enjoy his oats or walk round a paddock?'

This she refused to answer, though, and he sighed. 'All right. We'll leave that for now. Let's talk about you. It's perfectly understandable for you to be feeling like you are, Katie-bug! After your father's influence for years, you can't expect to leave and be blithely happy the next day. This is all new and probably very scary for you, isn't it? Right?' He persisted when she wouldn't answer.

At last she met his eyes and she nodded faintly. 'I feel like a fool,' she muttered.

'Why? Because you're acting perfectly human? Because you're admitting a weakness to someone else?' he asked her shrewdly.

'Because,' she admitted reluctantly, 'I've never cried all over somebody before this.' She wiped her eyes and stared at him in consternation as he threw back his head and laughed. 'I didn't realise that my tears were a source of amusement,' she commented acidly.

'Love, I'm not laughing at you!' he told her, still chuckling. 'If you could see Jana when she loses one of her cats! Sometimes they take off for who knows where, probably heading for home, and she cries buckets all over me and Marian and all the other nutty animals in the kitchen! I have had,' he ended mildly, 'some experience, you see.'

She was regarding him with just a hint of amusement. 'You wear it well,' she remarked. His eyes danced.

'I do, don't I? But don't tell Jana that I told you, all right? I'm sure that you'll find out soon enough for yourself.'

'Why?' she asked suddenly. She stared down into his eyes as he crouched before her. 'I mean, why are you doing this for me? Why should you care? I still don't understand you!'

This time, it was he who lowered his eyes away from hers. He was silent as if in thought, and then he started to speak very slowly. 'When I first saw you, everything about you was vibrant,' he said softly. 'Your hair danced, your lips quirked in laughter at the whole stupid, boring party, and your eyes had little devils lurking in them, peeping out and making me want to laugh out loud. I hate to see anything go to waste, and your life seemed like such a special thing, that no one else was fully appreciating. Not even you appreciated it, I could see, and then I started to sense some things that made me uneasy. Can you understand when I say that suddenly I wanted nothing more than to see you happy, as everyone has a right to be? That it didn't have anything to do with what was between your father and me? I suppose it sounds pretty lame to you, doesn't it?'

She gave a tiny shrug, feeling inside a special glow from his open disclosure. 'If you had caught me a little while ago, when I didn't have a clue as to any other lifestyle but the one I was leading, I would have said that it sounded lame. But Marian fusses over a complete stranger—that's me, you know—and Jana cries over cats, and I cry for a fat old pony.' She paused. 'I think that I am beginning to understand you. I'm glad I'm beginning to understand you. What I wonder is,' she continued, her eyes reflective, 'just what in the world could produce anything like my father? He's positively inhuman!'

Luke stood and strolled over to his seat, picking up his glass and draining it. 'While you're asking that, you might as well ask why there are such selfish people as the group your father associates with, or how can a person have the disposition of a killer, and why are there wars in the world, and why not plenty of food for all the starving people?' he replied to her query. 'And,' he continued mildly, 'if you find out any of the answers, let me know. I'd like to hear some myself.'

She smiled, the first smile that day and the lighting up of her face caused him to look at her as if he could not look away. 'I've been a foolish, immature person,' she commented matter-of-factly, 'and I rather enjoyed crying on your shoulder since it was quite a novel experience for me! Now why are you laughing like that?'

He only shook his head in reply, and asked instead, 'Is your pride up to accepting the idea of a vacation until you feel ready to hunt for a job? In the meantime, I'll be on the lookout for you.'

She said hesitantly, 'I'd like that—to have some time to think, I mean. But do you think that I might be able to borrow some money from you until I start receiving a pay-check? It would be strictly a loan.'

A slow smile lit up his dark face. 'Do you mean to tell me that you left home without a cent?' he asked.

'I did leave my chequebook,' admitted Katherine sheepishly. 'On purpose. I didn't want to take anything from home that I didn't absolutely need.'

'Pride, or pique?' he enquired, watching her face speculatively. She coloured under his gaze.

'I prefer to think of it as idealism,' she murmured. 'It was probably a stupid gesture, because I had quite a bit of money from last month's allowance, but I wanted to leave and be able to say that I really did make it on my own. Of course, I'm not really. I mean, I'm staying here and eating your food, and all. But if I pay you back, then I really did make it, didn't I?'

At this muddled speech for some reason he looked pleased, but she refrained from asking him just what he was thinking, and after a bit he said, 'We'll consider any actual cash a loan, all right?' She nodded and he continued, 'But I will not, repeat, will not accept any money for letting you stay here, do you understand? Not do I want money for the food you've consumed! No—don't argue with me, Kate! That would be an insult to my hospitality. And please don't feel yu have to look for another place to live because that is ridiculous when we have so much room here. We aren't even taking up half of the bedrooms upstairs! If you absolutely must do something to earn your keep, then ask Marian if she needs any help with the cooking, or something.'

'But,' she said sheepishly, 'I can't cook.'

He laughed. 'Then learn.'

Katherine nursed her burnt fingers the next afternoon, and swore in disgust. The terrible-smelling stuff stuck in the bottom of the small saucepan was supposed to have been a cheese sauce. It in no way resembled a substance that could be construed as edible. Marian wandered over from her languid position at the table to peer enquiringly over Katherine's shoulder. 'Oh, my,' she murmured, awestruck.

'Here, dear, let me get some cream for your fingers,' she said tactfully, as Katherine's brow began to darken. 'Do you think they'll blister?'

'Probably,' she said gloomily. 'And I'm going to be a virtual cripple, with my other hand all bandaged up!' Her face began to clear up. 'Do you think that Luke'll take us out to dinner, now that I've thoroughly ruined ours?'

'You haven't "thoroughly ruined" dinner yet,' Marian grimly retorted. 'Just because the pork chops are a little dark and tough, and the mashed potatoes are a tiny bit lumpy, doesn't mean that we are giving up!'

'Those pork chops are practically in cinders,' she grumbled, wincing at the pressure that Marian was applying to her tender fingers. 'And the potatoes look ghastly. The only thing not messed up is the salad, and what can you do to ruin a salad, for heaven's sake? What are we going to have for dessert now?'

Marian went to the pantry and rummaged around thoughtfully. 'We could have some fruit cocktail,' she called over her shoulder. 'There are several cans in here. It's not the most elegant dessert, but if we add some freshly cut apples and some orange slices, I think we'll make do.'

'Couldn't you whip up something kind of nice, and let me toss the pork chops and potatoes,' she pleaded hopefully. 'I cringe at the thought of serving it to Jana and Luke!' Marian looked at her wryly. 'Oh, you know what I mean! After all, you've messed up dinners before, haven't you?'

'Lord, yes,' she said calmly. 'And I know that the best way to learn to cook is when you have to eat your mistakes. It makes you try harder the next time, you know. Besides, you insisted at the breakfast table this morning that you wanted to prepare dinner, and everyone agreed. So, this is dinner!' She smiled at Katherine's hot and flushed face. 'It will be edible, dear, and nobody will mind. After all, you are just learning, and everyone knows it.'

When the four of them sat down to dinner, though, Katherine couldn't help but feel embarrassed at the potatoes and chops. However, the salad looked attractive, with tomatoes and green peppers and freshly fried bacon bits in it, and there was a loaf of (store bought, but good) french bread toasting in the oven and smelling aromatic, and the fruit cocktail with the fresh apples and oranges tasted delicious when she'd sampled it experimentally.

Everyone tucked into the serving dishes: Marian wearing her dry smile, Katherine with a slight blush, and Jana and Luke making a great show of polite eagerness. The conversation was delightful, as Jana chattered non-stop about her volunteer work at the hospital. Katherine tried and tried to cut into her dark, hard pork chop, but her painful fingers and awkwardly bandaged hand prevented much success. After managing to get a few bites into her mouth, she finally said in disgust, 'Marian, eating one's mistakes may be all right when you're talking about humble pie, but this pork chop is beyond redemption!' She looked around at everyone's plate. Luke was struggling manfully with half of his chop to go, and Marian was caught red-handed with a piece of meat offered to the pup, Oliver, who was waiting patiently under the table. Jana's had not been touched. In fact, as she looked around she also noticed that nobody had eaten their salad portions either.

'What's wrong with the salad?' she asked suspiciously, picking up her fork and digging into her own. Luke's face was red as he appeared to choke, Jana clucked unhappily and Marian looked mystified. She put a forkful into her mouth and nearly gagged. 'Vinegar!' she gasped, reaching for her water-glass frantically. As she gulped the water, Luke put his darkened face into one huge hand.

'What?' asked Marian confusedly. She picked up her fork also, and tentatively tried a morsel of her own salad. The expression on her face was ludicrous in its dismay. 'Oh, Katherine! You got the oil and the vinegar proportions mixed up, and added too much vinegar!'

She looked around the table, at the terrible mashed potatoes, the beautiful, ruined salad, and her dinner companions. Luke's shoulders were shaking silently, and Jana seemed to have difficulty in controlling her breathing. Marian's eyes were brimming, and then that lady put her head up, sniffing suspiciously, 'Do you smell anything?'

'My bread!' wailed Katherine, and she shot out of her chair to run into the kitchen. The burning smell was stronger in that room, and she frantically opened the oven door to see a blackened log sitting on a flat metal sheet, smoking faintly. Snatching up a tea towel, she grabbed at the burning mess and ran for the sink, jiggling the hot metal sheet back and forth. She threw it into the sink. By that time the others had reached the door to the kitchen, and she could hear Luke and Marian roaring with laughter and Jana trying to shush them up in between giggles of her own. The three, in turn, saw Katherine standing with her back to the door, one arm passed around the front of her waist and one hand pressed to cover her face with her head bent and hair swinging forward. Her shoulders were shaking convulsively.

'Kate!' Luke bounded forward and put his arm round her quivering shoulders. She didn't make a sound, and all three tried desperately to control their laughter.

'Don't take it so badly, honey!' Jana crooned, also coming up to her. She patted the bright bent head. 'It's only bread. You shouldn't feel we're laughing at you. It's just—just——' Her eyes met her brother's over Katherine's head and she dissolved into splutters.

'Come on, Katherine!' Marian scolded affectionately. 'We're only indulging in a bit of humour! It doesn't mean anything serious. Love, if you could have seen your face when you tried that awful salad, you would be in stitches too!'

Katherine threw back her head and gasped for air. Her eyes were streaming with tears and at first the other three looked at each other, aghast at the reaction their laughter had evoked. Then a delicious peal of mirth burst forth from her, and she doubled up in a spasm. 'Oh!' she gasped. 'Oh, ooohhh! If you could have seen your faces; if you could see your faces now!' Her head came up and she met Luke's stunned eyes. 'You looked like you were going to die from choking! And you,' her large, sparkling, gleeful eyes, still streaming with tears, turned to Jana, 'you tried so hard to keep from eating by talking on and on!' Everyone started to chuckle as they stared at her. 'And your face, Marian, when you tried the salad was too, too much ....' She fell into Luke's arms, still chortling with glee. 'Help me to a chair!'

When they had all managed to quieten down, Katherine asked, 'Would you think it's possible to send out for a pizza? I, er, didn't get enough to eat.'

'Possible! You've got to be joking,' Luke told her feelingly. 'I can't think of any other alternative.'

In a relatively short time, with the combined efforts of the three women, the mess from the uneaten meal was cleared up and the food disposed of, much to the satisfaction of all concerned, especially the animals. Luke left to pick up the pizza he'd ordered and, after resetting the table and waiting for him to arrive, they all sat down to a perfectly delicious meal complete with wine and candlelight. The mood was mellow as everyone disposed of the fruit cocktail at the end.

'I've never,' Jana remarked, licking her spoon happily, 'had a more enjoyable meal, and can't remember having seen you laugh before this, Katherine! Am I glad you took the whole thing so well!'

'Oh well,' she sighed, her laughing eyes travelling over everyone and alighting on Luke. 'I can only hope that next time I do better. However, I promise not to subject anyone to eating something that they violently object to!'

For the next several days, she spent her time either trying to bake various foods, or reading. Every day she took a leisurely walk, sometimes waiting for Luke to get home from work so that he could accompany her and sometimes getting out by herself. She was noticing a difference in herself, a quality that she had never seen before, and it was several days before she could put a name to just what it was.

She was smiling more easily and more openly without the mockery that had once been so evident. She had even begun to laugh out loud more than she ever had before. Most of all, though, the difference was seen in her eyes, for her habitual expression, as it had always been, was quiet and serious. But the difference was that now her eyes twinkled.

However, the change that she was most struck by was that she found herself spending more time with books and dwelling on a particular theme for quite a while. She was able to sit for longer periods, finding that she did not need strenuous physical exercise any more to relieve her tensions. Many evenings she would spend with Luke reading a book, or while he worked on papers brought home from work she would idly sketch or watch television. In short, Katherine was learning to be quiet.

She loved to spend time with Marian in the kitchen and found herself making very passable meals, to the surprise of Luke and the delight of Jana. Many times she put a dessert in to bake and sat down with a hot drink to ask Marian questions about herself. She found that the older woman had a particular talent for describing places she had visited and impressions that people left her with. Marian was also a shrewd judge of character, and an intelligent, discerning reader. When Katherine found out that she had a degree in English, she was considerably surprised.

'But why,' she asked Marian one rainy afternoon, 'are you content with being a housekeeper?'

'And what is wrong with being a housekeeper?' retorted Marian, with mock outrage. She regarded Katherine with a faint smile, her lined hands cupping the hot mug of tea that she sipped from time to time. 'What happened to me,' she continued, 'is that I took a subject that I love and found that I didn't want it for a job, I wanted it to remain fun, and so, I found something that I do very well, and that leaves me a terrific amount of time for my own interests. You see, I like housework. And I love Jana and Luke. Both of them have been very good to me, treating me as if I'm part of the family—why, hello, love.'

Jana walked through the kitchen and said absently, 'What do you mean, "like you're part of the family", you nut? You are family.' She scratched the puppy behind the ear and disappeared.

After Katherine had taken out a beautifully brown pie, she went thoughtfully to her quiet corner in the library to think. She had postponed thinking about the search for a job, because the idea was very uncomfortable to her. Now, for the first time, she examined the reason why. It quite suddenly struck her that she was afraid that she wouldn't find a job good enough for her. This incredible realisation stayed with her for some time. In the past she had always been accustomed to being in the limelight. Everything she had done or accomplished had been to attract attention to herself, from the spectacular and flashy way she rode horses and played tennis down to the clothes she wore. When she started a project, she dug into it with a singlemindedness that sooner or later placed her in front of all the others. When she had acted the individualist at any of the social gatherings she had attended, it was, of course, to set herself apart from the ordinary. Now she saw, what she feared was the commonplace.

It was a very quiet Katherine that looked up into the smiling and enquiring eyes of Luke, newly home from work.

CHAPTER SIX

'YOU certainly seem to have developed a liking for that spot,' he remarked whimsically, loosening his tie and throwing his jacket carelessly on to a nearby chair. 'Do you think you will nest there?'

She smiled. 'It's a thought. Do you have any ideas of what I could build my nest with? Twigs and grass might make a mess on the carpet.'

His teeth flashed in response. 'Do you think a warm blanket and perhaps a pillow might do the trick?' Sitting down with his long legs stretched out in front of him, he sighed gustily. 'That feels good.'

She regarded him soberly, taking in the lines of tiredness and the ruffled hair, the air of exhaustion, the lax hands. 'What would you like to drink?' she offered. 'I'll go and get you something.'

'Mmm. How about a glass of orange juice with a touch—just a touch, mind you—of vodka?' he murmured, closing his eyes. She jumped to her feet.

'Be right back.' When she came into the room again, she was carrying two glasses full of an iced drink and she handed one to him. He sat up a little and murmured thanks as he sipped it.

'Where are the others?' he asked curiously.

'Marian's making supper—her turn tonight, so you can relax,' she drily told him, and was rewarded with a chuckle. 'Jana's out walking Oliver somewhere.' After a pause, she asked him, 'Tell me, Luke, why are you doing what you're doing? Are you very rich?'

'And,' he enquired lazily, regarding her through half-closed eyes, 'which one do I answer first? Yes, I am considered wealthy, although not as wealthy as your father, and I like what I do. Satisfied?'

'You know I'm not,' was her quiet reply.

'Oh Lordy. You actually *want* me to get philosophical at the end of the day?' He sighed. 'All right. I do what I do because I've built up a line of hotels that are excellent and efficient. It takes a good deal of work to keep them going. I started the chain because I like to build things, and to promote projects. I suppose it didn't have to be hotels. I suspect I may want to do something else with my life. Thankfully, I'm in a financial position now to consider just about anything, but you can be sure that it will be some kind of venture that somehow involves planning, organisation and some type of building—either physically or a structured establishment like a new company.' He took a sip of his drink and shrugged. 'Who knows what the future might bring?' He grinned at her. 'I can just see the little ideas clicking in your tiny mind!'

'Beast,' she muttered at this, but it was an absent-minded sally, and she shifted in her seat. 'I've been thinking about what I want to do with myself,' she confessed, a little forlornly. 'I don't know what I want to do! I can't do anything!'

'That sounds very pathetic,' he observed. Then he quickly added, 'Don't get so defensive, now! We'll work this out, and then maybe you'll feel better about things.'

'Marian is so intelligent and she enjoys house-keeping, and you like what you're doing, and Jana . . . well, I'm not sure what she *does*, but she just *is*, and——'

'Stop,' he commanded quietly, and she did. He said, 'What did you just say about Jana?'

'I said that she just is,' repeated a bewildered Katherine. He nodded at her as if to say, 'Well?' and she frowned in confusion. Finally she said, 'I don't get what you're trying to say to me.'

'My dear girl, *I* 'm not trying to say anything to you,' he replied mildly. 'You've said it all.' Luke sat up and started to talk. 'Kate, don't expect me to tell you what you want or what you need out of life. You've got to figure that out for yourself. If you did but know it, you have just said what a lot of people spend years scrabbling around in the mud, so to speak, to find out.'

'All I said was that Jana just exists as herself,' she replied a little peevishly, 'and I don't know what a big deal that is . . . oh! I see.' Her eyes weren't focusing as she thought deeply. 'Just be yourself and—and whatever you do you will be happy.'

'To a great extent, yes.' He smiled. 'Of course, at some time or another, one has to work at different jobs and work round to attaining whatever it is one wants, but truly happy people get there sooner or later. What is it you want to be, Katie?'

The question, so easily and casually spoken, had her replying to it as easily, and unthinkingly she gave him the answer that she had agonised over for the past week. 'Why, I suppose I want to be useful since I've never been *that* before, and I guess I want to be needed, too. I want to be giving and caring like Jana and Marian and—you.' She couldn't, for some reason, meet his eyes.

When a hand came and covered hers with a soft touch, she started and brought her eyes up to his face to see a most tender expression on his lean face. 'You have made Jana smile when you walk into a room,' he said quietly. 'You have made me want to come home in the evenings more than I've wanted to for a long time.' Her eyes stayed with him, entranced. 'You give a little puppy a warm place to rest on your lap and a gentle pat on the head as you pass, making him watch you with those big adoring eyes. You can make Marian laugh as I've never seen her laugh before. Will you believe me when I say that you are needed?'

Her eyes dropped; she didn't know how to reply. The careful hand came to her cheek and stroked it in a fleeting caress. 'Kate.' The use of her name, so simply spoken, had her eyes returning to his again, like a small bird winging home. 'You underrate yourself so terribly. You trust me?' She nodded. 'Then trust this: you are needed.' And with those words, he brought his dark head to her slowly. Her eyelids fluttered and closed, and she felt a soft, soft touch brush her lips once, twice, and then her cheek.

'Well!' said an extremely interested voice from the direction of the doorway. Katherine started violently, and Luke moved away. They both looked at the speaker, the one with a slight smile on his face and the other with a blush. Marian stood regarding them with a wide, wide smile. 'Dinner,' she announced impressively, 'is served.'

At the end of another quiet evening, Luke walked up the staircase with Katherine and paused at her door, smiling down at her. His shirt was open several buttons and rather thick hair was to be seen in the shadow of his chest. Both hands were resting in an easy manner on his slim waist, and his feet were slightly apart as if he were balanced against a wind. His black hair fell over his brow and nearly into his dancing eyes. 'Would you like me to ask around to see what sort of job I can get you, or would you prefer to do it yourself?' he asked.

She shrugged. 'I would like to look around, but if you have any suggestions or possibilities, please let me know,' was her reply. He nodded, and yet made no move to walk away. She muttered, embarrassed, 'Er, if you don't mind, I'll go to bed now.' She watched the pretty blue carpet intently.

'How would you like to go out tomorrow evening?' was his answer. Her eyebrows shot up in surprise, as did her head.

'And do what?' she queried blankly, making him laugh.

'Anyone would think that you've never been on a date before,' he teased. She shook her head in protest at this, but her eyes returned his smile, her cheeks faintly pink. 'What would you like to do? Go out for supper? Maybe catch a movie, or perhaps visit a nightclub and go dancing?' His tone, as was his expression, was indulgent.

'Dancing,' she decided with delight. 'I just love to dance!'

'All right, I'll make reservations at a restaurant, and atfer we eat we can see where to go from there,' he suggested. There was another pause as they looked at each other. She felt troubled in some way, vaguely disturbed, and the uneasiness showed in the back of her eyes. His expression was unreadable to her, and she tried to fathom what he was thinking. He looked almost brooding. As if he could not stop himself, one hand came up slowly and captured a handful of her bright, silken hair. He knotted his hand into a fist, clenching the strands, and then he tugged gently. The movement was not alarming; she knew that if she had wanted to she could have pulled out of his grasp easily. But she found she didn't want to. She found herself going forward willingly, and as he bent his head very carefully, she raised her lips to his.

The warm, soft touch of his lips caused her to press hers to his more firmly, and she felt his arms going round her, holding her tightly. Her arms slid around his strong muscled neck. All she could think of was how utterly safe, how completely cherished she felt, with those hard arms holding her so carefully. She had been kissed before, but how insipid those embraces now seemed! The other times she had put up with the charade, intent only on getting into the house and knowing that her apparent interest in her escort was all a sham. But this was real. She was responding to him of her own volition.

And then it changed. She felt the passion in him, and those careful arms tightened until she felt her ribs would snap. The soft touch on her lips hardened, and demanded her open mouth. The long legs took her weight as he pulled her more completely against him, and she felt the hard muscles of his thighs. She jerked her head away with a painful wrench as a sudden, inexplicable fear coursed through her.

'Let go of me!' she gasped, straining her neck and head away. In response, his hold only tightened and for an agonising moment she couldn't breathe. Then she was let go and she nearly fell against the closed door of her room in reaction. She kept her face turned away for fear of showing just how completely her composure was ruined. Her knees, she noticed with an odd detachment, were trembling.

He moved, although she couldn't see his action with her head bent and eyes averted, but something made her turn and raise her eyes to him. He was standing with his back to her, one hand at the back of his neck as he stared up, dark hair falling back, and the other one again at his waist. She stared at his back for a few moments, noticing almost unwillingly how his shoulders were much broader than his hips, and how the powerful line of his back spoke of powerful muscles underneath the shirt. She wondered crazily if his legs had as much hair on them as his chest, and shied away from the thought.

Just then he turned his head and regarded her from under lowered brows, his face stern and unsmiling. His eyes widened as he took in her own huge eyes with the strange alarm set in the darkened green. 'I'm sorry,' he said abruptly. 'It won't happen again.' With that, he strode down the hall and disappeared into his own room. He didn't see her hand half lifted to him in a tentative, silent denial, nor did he notice her shoulders droop in a dejected slump as she quietly opened her own door and went inside. She was hard put to explain the dejection herself.

The next morning, she rose late, and by the time she was downstairs there was no chance of seeing Luke before he went to work. She didn't know if she was happy or sad about that.

Marian and Jana were enjoying a comfortable talk when she entered the kitchen. She helped herself to a glass of milk and popped some bread in the toaster, and then sat down with the other woman.

Jana grinned at her impishly. 'Luke told me to tell you that he made a reservation for two at the Regency,' she commented carelessly, and then abandoned the role of a disinterested messenger, and asked her happily, 'Oh, Katherine, what are you going to wear? He said to be ready by eight.'

She smiled at this as Marian grumbled, 'Wish someone would take me out once in a while!'

'Are you going dancing?' Jana asked her. 'Good heavens, I haven't been dancing in years!'

'Come on,' Katherine protested laughingly. 'It can't be that long. You aren't old enough! You are certainly attractive enough!'

'My dear,' Jana replied with a smile, 'just how old do you think I am?'

'Well, I don't know,' she shrugged. Her eyes

searched Jana's amused face. 'I know that you're older than Luke, and that he's—what, thirty-five, -six?'

'Eight, love,' Marian put in with a grin. 'Luke is thirty-eight, although you'd never tell by looking at him.

She was quite shocked at this and couldn't help exclaiming, 'Good God! Why, then,' she turned her eyes to Jana, 'you've got to be around ... forty?' Jana's smile grew larger, and Marian chuckled softly. 'Forty-one? Come on, you're pulling my leg! Forty-two? You can't be any older than forty-three! I won't believe it!'

'I am,' Jana stated with a great show of satisfaction, 'forty-nine, as of last month. I'm eleven years older than Luke. He was, in a quaint term, an "accident" that turned our mother's hair completely grey, and had our father going to an early grave.'

Later, as she was up in her room and washing her hair, Katherine couldn't help but be depressed on thinking over the conversation of that morning. She had no idea that Luke was so much older than she, and kept thinking how young she must appear to all of them. She must seem so immature to him! The problems that had once been monumental to her, an unsurmountable obstacle, must have been tiringly childish to him. And when her thoughts turned, inevitably, to the events of the night before, she almost cringed with embarrassment.

In this discouraged and dejected mood, she started to ready herself for her evening out. She went down the hall, having asked Jana earlier if she could borrow her steam curler set, and stayed to ask her advice on the dress she was going to wear. 'It's not,' she told Jana with a touch of sarcasm, 'as if I have so many choices, but do you think this will do?' Holding up for

inspection a dark gold dress that had a bit of shine to
its slinky material, she searched the older woman's
face for approval.

'Very nice,' Jana replied, coming over to finger it
with an appreciative hand. 'Hold it up in front of
you—there, like that. You know, it's just the right
colour for you. It seems to bring out all the gold lights
and the reddish colour in your beautiful hair. Go and
put it on, love, and by the time you get back here the
curlers should be hot enough. I'll help you roll up
your hair, if you want.'

Katherine did want, and she hurried down the hall
to slip on the dress. The silky material caressed her
skin and slipped into place with a little rustle. The
shoulder straps were thin, and the neckline low. There
was practically no back at all to the dress, and though
the front was thick enough, she knew that there could
be no mistake about whether she was wearing a bra or
not. She stopped long enough to put on a pair of filmy
thin tights that lent a glistening silver sheen to her
slender legs. Then she grabbed her pair of gold
sandals and hurried back to Jana's room.

She paused for a moment on the threshold, a slim
and yet delicately rounded young woman, with fine
graceful lines to her long legs and a way of walking
that had Jana's eyes following her bemusedly as she
crossed the room with a fluid motion. Katherine stood
in front of the other woman quietly, turning once for
good effect. 'Will it do?' she asked anxiously, hurrying
the turn so that she could glance at Jana's face. That
lady laughed and hurried over to give her a tight hug.

'Will it do! My dear, you look absolutely delightful!'
Jana took Katherine into her own private bathroom.
'I'll just roll your hair up for you, and then you can
run off and put on a little make-up while the curlers
cool and your hair sets.'

Cunningly applied blusher emphasised her high cheekbones even more strikingly, and her eyelids, stroked with a distinctive gold-brown shadow, made her green eyes glow vividly. Black mascara, a touch of eyeliner, and a bronze lipstick glazing her well-shaped lips completed her toilette. She quickly unrolled the cold curlers and brushed her abundant hair briskly. After shaking her head violently, she threw her hair back and surveyed it critically. It would do. A few squirts of hairspray to help hold it in place, and she was quite ready.

A knock sounded at her door. 'How does a glass of sherry sound before we leave?' a deep voice vibrated through the closed doors, reaching, she felt, to her bones.

As she opened the door and looked him full in the face, his voice faded into silence. They stared at each other for a long, long time. She seemed to be having trouble with her breathing. That's a strange way for him to be affecting me, she thought dazedly. She looked him up and down, taking in the black, slim-fitting suit with the slightly shimmery grey shirt and black tie, and the sleek well-brushed hair. There was a faint blue tinge to his brown skin along the jawline that would never go away after shaving. Her eyes travelled back to his expressionless face. He was looking white.

'Are you all right?' she felt urged to ask. He shook his head impatiently, looking very suddenly quite normal.

'Of course I am. Don't I look all right?' was his reply, as he backed away from her door to let her past him into the hall. She could have replied to that with a very positive, vehement affirmation, but merely contented herself with a slight nod.

Downstairs, he let her precede him into the library

where the two women sat, sipping small glasses of amber liquid. Both turned at the pair's entrance. 'Oh, my dear!' Marian exclaimed approvingly. 'You look positively enchanting! Doesn't she look lovely, Luke?'

'Yes,' he replied, moving over to a low cabinet with two full glasses sitting on it. He picked up both, handing one to Katherine before drinking from his own. She murmured her thanks and sipped appreciatively. Then she moved over to the large leather couch to sit at the edge closest to the other women, crossing her slim legs with an easy grace. She glanced quickly at Luke and found him staring straight ahead of himself, apparently at nothing, and sipping his sherry with a peculiar rigid expression. She turned back to Jana to listen to what that lady was telling her.

'Oh, Katherine, I almost forgot to ask you! Did you remember that you asked me to make an appointment at the hospital for the removal of your stitches? (What a pity your hand is bandaged tonight, dear!) Well, when I was at the hospital this afternoon, I overheard that the personnel department will be accepting applications tomorrow for positions as nurses' aides, and I immediately thought of you! Of course, you would probably have a much more exacting role than that of a mere volunteer! I was just wondering if you might possibly be interested in something like that?'

'What a splendid idea!' Katherine said, smiling dazzlingly at Jana and Marian, the beauty of which made both ladies blink. 'Do you know, that might be just the thing for me! I probably wouldn't want to make it a career, but it would certainly be the right start. Oh, Jana, I think I would like to apply! When did you manage to make my appointment for?'

'Two o'clock tomorrow afternoon. It'll just take five minutes to get the stitches taken out, and then we can go to the personnel department and you can fill in your application form while I go on to work. I'm supposed to be there at two-thirty. Would you mind driving back to the house in my car, and coming back for me at six-thirty?'

'Oh no, of course not!' she instantly replied, her eyes travelling over Marian without really seeing her. She was wrapped up in sudden possibilities, but her eyes came back quickly to Jana. 'But what if they don't hire me? I mean, I have no experience whatsoever, and can think of no reason why they should! I think I'm getting a little depressed at the thought!'

'No problem,' Jana smiled at her, as she airily waved away this minor difficulty. Her blue eyes rested on Katherine kindly. 'Just put me down as a personal reference, dear. They'll hire you.'

'But——' she began, protesting at this blithe assurance, until she saw the look in Jana's eyes. 'Oh.' She paused a moment. 'I see.'

'Do you, love? You see, I've been very good to the Memorial Hospital in Frankfort, both with my time and especially with my money. Yes,' her eyes twinkled at Katherine, 'I think you do see, after all.'

'Katie-bug.' Luke's voice was very quiet, but she heard him immediately, and turned to look at him. He regarded her face thoughtfully. 'Perhaps we should be leaving, since the reservation is for eight-thirty,' he suggested. She rose quickly and put her empty glass on the tray nearby. He ran an eye down her slim frame. 'Do you have an evening wrap?'

'Oh, do you think I need one?' she asked in dismay. 'I didn't think to bring one from home, and it's been so warm for July.'

'It is supposed to cool off quite a bit tonight,' he said, and turned to Jana. 'Would you mind lending Katherine your sable jacket for tonight, love?'

'Of course not!' She was already on her feet. 'My very thought, Luke. I'll be right down with it.'

After Jana had pressed the meltingly soft fur coat into Katherine's reluctant hands, they said their good nights to the two women, Luke telling them that it was possibly going to be very late before they returned.

He was silent as he handed her into the low-slung sports car, and later when he drove unsmilingly through the streets. She ventured a few glances his way, wondering at his strangely unapproachable mood, but said nothing.

When he pulled into the car park of the well-known and quietly elegant restaurant, Katherine was more nervous by his silence that she would have been comfortable to admit. She gladly got out of the car and draped the sable jacket around her shoulders while Luke stood near, watching. He asked her, 'Ready?' and she nodded, vaguely noticing the arrival of a dark saloon car that parked not far away.

Luke put a hand under her right elbow and walked with her to the entrance of the restaurant, moving forward and opening the door for her politely and passing through after her. He left her for a moment to announce their arrival while she, having been to the restaurant before, went to a dark corner that surprisingly led to a hall with a public phone, the cloakrooms, and a lit doorway which was the coat room. She handed the jacket to the quick attendant with a murmured thanks and took the ticket he gave her in return. As she turned back to go down the semidark hall, she bumped hard into a large bulk. She looked up with a politely phrased apology and found herself staring into the eyes of a stranger, who looked considerably startled and almost thrust her aside to hurry down the hall. She stared after the man reflectively and with some astonishment, and only belatedly remembering that Luke must be waiting for her in the restaurant's foyer. She turned and hurried back the way she had come.

He was standing in conversation with a vivacious-looking little brunette who was talking and gesturing animatedly. Just as she rounded the corner, he looked up, a tall, straight figure in black, with his proud-looking head still a little inclined towards the pretty woman by his side to whom he had been listening. His dark eyes met hers and he smiled. The brunette, catching sight of Katherine walking their way with her long, graceful, compelling stride, seemed to melt away out of existence. Katherine never spared the girl a glance, and Luke moved forward to take her slender bare arm in his warm and easy grasp.

'Our table's ready,' he murmured in her ear, and they both moved to the floor where the tables were tastefully arranged to give the illusion of separateness and privacy to each. They stood poised just for a moment in the frame of the arched doorway, the one figure dark and almost broodingly handsome, and the other like a living flame. Then, as they saw where the hostess was leading them, both moved simultaneously forward with a fluidity and grace, and a natural continuity in their movements that had heads turning, looking, watching them pass. Katherine was by no means disconcerted by the obvious attention that she and Luke were receiving. This type of recognition was something that she was very used to, and in fact would have missed if it had not been there. A slight smile hovered around her full, beautifully formed lips, but other than that she ignored the other tables.

The hostess led them to a rather more secluded table than the others, and Katherine sank into the chair that Luke held for her with a smile of thanks. He pulled out the other and sat down also, smiling his first real smile of the evening full into her receptive eyes. It was quite something; he could turn on enough charm to coax a badger out of its hole if he wanted to. It made her blink.

'You know,' he said softly, his eyes twinkling, 'you quite disappointed me back there.'

This made her blink. 'Back where?' she asked in confusion. 'I didn't mean to do anything.'

'Don't worry,' he said, starting to laugh a little. 'It wasn't intentional, I know.' He looked into her mystified eyes for a minute, and then relented. 'I was expecting a rather different reaction when you saw that precious little brunette, but to my surprise you didn't even acknowledge the girl's existence! You didn't have any curiosity as to who she was?'

She looked amused. 'Okay, who was she?' she asked obligingly.

He threw back his head and laughed harder. 'Love, I have no idea! She just came up to me and started talking!'

'It's just as I thought,' she shrugged it away, tossing her gleaming hair behind one shoulder. 'Nobody important to me.'

'Now you *have* disappointed me!' he shook his head despairingly. 'I was hoping for some show of jealousy in those green eyes, some little indication of emotion! You've broken my sorry heart, Katie.' As she laughed at Luke's welcome light-hearted change of mood and sent her eyes casually, idly around the occupants of the dining-room, she caught sight of the man who had bumped into her in the hall, his gaze upon her, his manner anything but casual. Alert, speculating, and sharp, yes, but not the gaze of a man merely admiring a good-looking and strange woman. Her eyes widened in surprise and some alarm, and she dropped them to her empty place-setting in consternation. Unless she was grossly mistaken, she had seen that man somewhere before. Just where, she couldn't place, but she had seen him somewhere.

'What is it?' Luke asked her sharply, catching sight of something in her face that evidently alarmed him, and he leaned forward to grasp her hand.

That brought her eyes back up, this time to look at him, and she replied quickly, 'Nothing! Nothing at all. I'm hungry, aren't you?' Her tone was light, but her eyes were troubled.

CHAPTER SEVEN

'DON'T give me that.' He was not, she saw, so easily put off, and his grip on her uninjured hand tightened. 'Tell me, Kate. What's troubling you?'

'It's really stupid,' she began in a low voice. Her eyes travelled away from his and started inspecting the table's furnishings. 'This fellow who bumped into me in the hall and quite rudely pushed me away even after I had apologised, is sitting just behind your left shoulder, alone, and he is staring at me very hard. It's just a little uncomfortable, that's all, no big deal.' Her eyes once again met his and found him reassuringly calm. 'Dumb?'

'Of course not. What does he look like?' he asked idly, releasing her hand and leaning back in his chair nonchalantly.

'It's the funniest thing, but I think I've seen him before—oh!' she exclaimed as she casually looked over to the table where the man had been sitting. She sat upright in astonishment. 'He's gone!' She quickly glanced all over the restaurant's dining-room, but he was nowhere to be found.

'Perhaps,' said Luke, sounding bored, 'he finished eating and left for the evening.'

She searched the table with her eyes and looked at him with the beginnings of frostiness. 'You think,' she said coldly, 'that I'm making all this up, don't you? I'm not. Why is there an open menu where he was sitting? Why should he leave in such a hurry?'

'I am most certainly not thinking that you have made all this up,' he replied with a maddening calm.

'And, I cannot guess why the fellow would get up and leave before eating. Perhaps he just changed his mind?'

Her green eyes threw silent and virulent sparks at him, which had the opposite effect that she wished: he smiled in amusement. 'Do you know,' she said reflectively, 'that I think you are being quite provokingly odious?'

He laughed outright. 'Come on, sweetheart, describe this menacing character to me and get him out of your mind once and for all,' he coaxed, his face open and relaxed. She caught the look in his eyes and started. Those eyes were anything but relaxed, and she must have stared too hard, because he lowered them instantly. 'Out with it, Katie-bug.'

She dispelled her uneasy feelings with a shrug, and started to describe the man to Luke. 'Well, he was dark—not as dark as you, mind, but more in a brown sort of way. He looked pretty big; when I bumped into him, it felt like I was running into a brick wall! His nose was a little battered-looking, like he'd been caught between a rock and a hard place, or should I say hard fist? He had a rather tough expression that could give you the shivers if you met him in a dark alley and you had something that he wanted.' Her voice trailed away.

'Observant chit, aren't you?' remarked Luke easily. 'He must've made an impression.'

'It's just,' she looked troubled, 'that I feel like I've seen him before, but can't quite remember where ... oh, forget it! Here comes our waiter. What are you going to have?'

After they had ordered, both relaxed with drinks. His was a whisky, and she sipped at a mixed fruit drink that was filled with crushed ice. 'You haven't been much from the house this last week, have you, poor Katie-bug?' Luke asked her sympathetically after taking a sip from his glass. When she looked into his eyes from over the rim of her own glass, she saw again that peculiar flash in them that made her wonder again at his strange, concealed intensity, but it was soon forgotten and she answered his light question easily.

'No, the only place I've been is in the back yard with Oliver,' she said, shaking her bright head at him in sadness. 'And, of course, the walks I've taken with you. It's been really nice, though. I have had the time to think, which I really needed. The weather's been so bad that I haven't had the least desire to play tennis! Do you play?' At his nod, she exclaimed excitedly, 'Why, splendid! You and I can play a few sets some time. I'm shockingly out of practice.'

'Oh, no,' was his disappointing response. 'I've heard about you. You play to kill. I don't think that I want to face such a ferocious opponent. You might hurt me.'

'Why, you wet noodle!' she expostulated with disgust. 'I wouldn't have credited you with such a timid outlook on life. You have very probably damaged my opinion of you beyond repair!' He smilingly retorted to that, and she stared at him, not bothering to answer for a minute. Then she said, 'You really wouldn't play with me?'

'Of course I will!' he assured her. 'I'm actually considered not so bad at the game myself!'

'At which remark I gather you play like the devil!' she concluded laughingly. The waiter interrupted their relaxed volley of insults as he served them the first course of what ended up being an excellent meal. After cheese and coffee, he asked her if she felt like working off the extensive damage she'd inflicted on her wand-like figure to which she remarked conversationally that she did, providing he was sure that he was up to such strenuous ventures. They left the restaurant in high good humour, to go to an exclusive club that he knew about but she'd never heard of, just north of Frankfort. She was pleasurably surprised to find the place well decorated and subdued in its lighting, and amazingly crowded for a Thursday evening.

'This place is popular,' she murmured in his ear, as he guided her to an empty spot with a small table to one corner, his arm holding her close.

He replied. 'Very. They have excellent entertainment here, and always engage fine musicians, whatever the particular musical style. There should be good dancing later on. Look, here comes the singer now.'

And so she sat back to enjoy sitting in the curve of Luke's warm encircling arm, and they spent a happy half-hour listening to the high-quality music. The woman who had come out on the small stage was not quite young but very beautiful, and she had a fine, carrying strong voice which Katherine found herself enjoying immensely.

There was a bad moment, when she sat forward, her eyes searching the surrounding crowd intently, her face white and strained.

'What is it?' he asked sharply, moving forward too and gazing at her face with concern. 'Kate, love, what's wrong?' She stared into his gaze, troubled, and shook her head.

'It's stupid!' He insisted however, and she murmured, feeling weak, 'Really, Luke, it's utter nonsense! I—it's just that I thought that I had seen that fellow again, over by the door. No, don't bother to look; whoever it really was, he's gone now. Please! Let's just change the subject, all right?' And with that, she refused to talk of it again that evening.

Later on, there was some dancing, and she was greatly pleased to find Luke an excellent partner for most dance styles, the only kind of dancing he refused being the really hard-paced, solitary gyrations that accompanied impossibly fast and loud music. It was the type, he said, that left him feeling as if he'd jumped around on a pogo stick for half an hour and was still bouncing about in a delayed reaction. At this, she had laughingly to sit out with him, which she certainly didn't mind—and she refused any invitations to walk out on the dance floor with other men although she was particularly good at that type of dancing herself.

The best part, she felt dreamily, as she put her head down on a very strong and receptive shoulder, was this: the slow, languorous dancing, with his arms around her holding her close, and the lights down low. His head was bent, and he had his face in her sweet-smelling hair. With a sigh of pure bliss, she closed her eyes and snuggled closer, feeling his arms tighten in response. She could feel the gentle rubbing of his thighs and the easy movement of his hips as they both swayed slightly, barely moving at all, merely using the chance to get close to each other. When the music stopped and the lights began to come up slowly, he whispered in her ear, 'Come on, love. Open your eyes. It's time for us to go now.'

She murmured, not lifting her head, 'But this feels so good, Luke. Just let me have a nice little nap here, and I'll be ready to go home in a minute—ouch! All right, I'm ready, I'm ready! Did you have to pinch?'

His only response was an absent-minded smile, and they were both silent as he contrived to negotiate a path through the door among the closely packed people. She collected Jana's coat at the door, and they left. She was glad of the coat when the cool, crisp air hit her exposed throat and legs. Luke turned the car's heater on when he started up, and soon the interior was cosy and refreshingly quiet after the bustle of the crowded nightclub. She fell asleep on the way home, after staring at Luke's strong profile a good portion of the way.

A light touch against her cheek and the draught of cold air had her opening her eyes to smile at him sleepily. The hand on her cheek stilled for a moment, and then was removed. He was a black silhouette against the light from the outside porch. 'Katie, you wouldn't like it if I let you stay in that uncomfortable position all night,' he whispered quietly, and she stirred with reluctance.

'I know,' she murmured, 'I'm coming.' She slid her legs out and stood up, into his arms. He held her for a long moment, and then let her go.

'I've got to put the car in the garage,' he said, handing her a key. 'That's to the front door—which reminds me. I'll have to get one for you to keep. Go on in, Katie-bug.'

She lingered. 'Would you like some coffee?' she offered. 'I'll be glad to make some for both of us.'

'Sure. Now hurry on in, and don't lock the door behind you! It's too cold for long conversations in that flimsy dress. Hurry up!' In spite of the fur coat that she wore over her shoulders, she felt a distinct chill as a breeze hit her exposed legs.

Two mugs were steaming and ready by the time he entered the kitchen, his hair tousled from the wind about his square, well-formed features. A sleepy Oliver sniffed half-heartedly at his heels for a few moments before returning to the big cardboard box which was stuffed with an old blanket and three cats, all of whom were sound asleep, supremely unconcerned at the various goings-on of the people they lived with. One did yawn hugely, showing a great set of very sharp-looking white teeth and a pointed little pink tongue, but no one noticed and the sleek little head was soon nestled back on curled furry paws.

'That was quick,' Luke commented, as he picked up the mug and sipped at it appreciatively. 'This is just right.'

She was seated at the table, minus her pretty shoes which she had left at the foot of the stairs for later retrieval. 'Mmm,' she replied, setting down her own mug. 'I didn't bother to heat the water to an undrinkable temperature.' She looked at her hands. 'Thank you for a wonderful evening, Luke, I loved every minute of it.'

He was smiling a little, and his eyes were soft as he regarded her over the rim of his mug. 'I enjoyed it, too. We'll do it again soon, all right?'

She nodded, flushing slightly. 'I'd like that.' He picked up her cup and took it over with his own empty one, depositing them for future washing, and then turned back.

'I'll walk you to your room,' he said softly. 'Come on.' She stood readily, and they walked slowly, arm in arm through the downstairs hall, stopping only for her to pick up her discarded shoes and dangle them from one hand. Neither spoke; theirs had been an evening of conversation, and further speech seemed unnecessary.

At the top of the stairs, in front of her bedroom door, he stopped and touched her just once with a quick finger. His lips formed the smiling, silent words, 'Good night. I'll see you tomorrow in the evening as I'm sure you will want to sleep in,' and he started to walk away from her, but he was stopped by her sudden detaining hand on his sleeve. He looked back, this time unsmilingly, and it took all her courage to drop her dangling shoes and go to him. She stood on tiptoe and put her two cold hands behind his neck. He did nothing to assist her, and it was she who had to gently apply pressure to bring his head down far enough so that she could plant a careful, lingering kiss on his warm lips.

That was enough to make him move, as quickly and as suddenly as she had moved to detain him, and he swept her into his arms for a crushing hug and a deep, searching kiss to which she responded wholeheartedly. This had been, after all, what she had wanted ever since the kiss from the night before. This time, she was not startled into any undue alarm. This time, it was he who broke away from the long kiss. He raised his head as if coming up for air, and then put his lips close to her ear, giving a quick kiss to that curving shell. 'I made you a promise last night that I didn't keep very well,' he whispered. She shook her head vehemently, causing him to start back away from her ear.

'I acted stupidly last night,' she whispered back, and smiled into his shadowed eyes. 'I wanted you to kiss me tonight.' Planting a kiss on her finger, she carried it to his straight lips and was rewarded with a gently planted kiss in the same spot. His arms loosened, and he stepped back. With a quick and suddenly shy smile, she backed away and went into her bedroom for the night.

Her newly opened eyes caught the pale gleam of the fresh early day. Her clock said exactly five minutes to six, and she slid out of bed to swing her hair back from her face and pad over to the wardrobe, drawing out her silk dressing-gown and belting it firmly about her. She was a bit surprised to find herself so wide awake after getting to bed around two in the morning, but she hadn't slept well all night and had awoken several times in the course of her sleep. One of her dreams, in which Luke figured prominently, had her wondering if he was awake yet or not. She opened her door and went downstairs, finding the kitchen dark and the front hall shadowed. Apparently no one else was up yet. Luke, she surmised, had most likely decided to catch an extra half-hour of sleep before a full day's work. Turning on the overhead kitchen light, she moved around quickly and prepared a full pot of coffee to brew. After that, she rummaged around for a tray and set it with one plate and silverware and two mugs. Then from the refrigerator she took two eggs and the wrapped package of bacon. While the bacon sizzled and the eggs slowly poached, she popped in bread to toast. Rescuing the bacon before it became too brown, she added the poached eggs on top of the buttered toast and covered the whole plate with a lid. The coffee was brewed and she poured two cups, adding to one enough cream for herself and to the other Luke's habitual teaspoonful of sugar.

Then, treading the stairs as carefully as she could, she travelled down the hall to the end door which was closed and opened it silently. What she saw made her nearly lose courage and take the breakfast back downstairs, for Luke was sprawled across the huge double bed, his chest bare and the golden skin rising and falling regularly. One arm encircled a pillow, and the other was flung straight out. About his hips was haphazardly strewn the top sheet, the only cover he was using. She saw the quilted bedspread kicked into a humped-up mess at the foot of the bed, and putting down the laden tray, she went forward to take it and pull it up to his chest, for she suspected that he didn't have anything on under the sheet. When she felt a little better with him covered up, she returned for the tray and set it on the bedside table. A quick look showed Luke's usually stern-looking countenance quite softened in sleep. He looked years younger with his hair tousled and a darkened chin from the stubble of an overnight beard. Her eyes traced the pattern of chest hairs as they swirled up and out from the middle, and she saw the wide, muscled strength in the rise and fall from his breathing. The lean, graceful fingers from the outflung arm curled up. She stuck out her own slim forefinger and inserted it into the half-covered palm of his upturned hand, tickling gently. Her eyes were on his face and when he opened his eyes to stare into her own, with no change of expression nor any other sign of having wakened, she found herself drinking in the soft, brilliant glow from those eyes. As she became aware of how she must look to him, with her long hair tumbled down her back and her dressing-gown belted carelessly about her, and especially the open, expressive look that must be in her eyes, she started to straighten up from her bent position and would have withdrawn her finger from the middle of his palm, but his hand tightened fast and she was imprisoned. He smiled at her, and the tenderness on his face together with the dark glow deep in his eyes had her sitting quite hard on the side of the bed, her knees feeling weak.

'I smell coffee,' he murmured sleepily, his own eyes travelling over her as if he could not see enough. His gaze moved to the table holding the laden tray, his finely curved nostrils quivering slightly. '... and—bacon? Did you fix me breakfast, Katie-bug?'

She wrinkled her nose at him. 'Yes, I did, and the eggs are poached just right, so I suggest that you hurry and eat them before it all cools.' He obligingly started to slide up into a sitting position, and as the covers slid down his chest and towards his hips, she averted her gaze and said jerkily, 'I'll be going now. Enjoy it.' She started to her feet to make good her statement, but again was thwarted by the quick grasp he laid on her arm.

'Don't,' he asked her. 'I see two mugs of coffee, and you must have intended one for yourself. Stay for a minute and drink your coffee with me.'

With her face turned away, she said with embarrassment, 'I don't really think I should, Luke.'

'Why not?' he asked, puzzled. Then, with a quick, comprehending laugh, he told her, 'I promise you that I'm perfectly respectable in my pyhjma bottoms.'

'Oh!' With that startled ejaculation, she swung her gaze round to see him throw back the covers and reveal low-slung, cotton pyjama trousers with a front white drawstring. Black hairs grew downwards and disappeared into the blue pyjamas, and she quickly looked up into his laughing face and then turned away, her face brick red. She mumbled, 'I only meant to leave you the tray and take my own cup to my room.'

'And I would appreciate your company so much more,' he coaxed her. A sharp-sounding buzz interrupted whatever he would have added to that, and he swung round to the opposite side of the bed to switch off his alarm. 'You were just about bang on time with that tray. What are you doing up so early, anyway?' he asked, and pulled his legs around to sit cross-legged on the bed. She handed his cup to him and took her own to sip.

'I just woke up. I didn't sleep very soundly last night, and when I saw what time it was, I decided to get up and surprise you.'

'A very nice surprise it is, too. Have a bacon slice.' He shared his breakfast with her as they sat and chatted together for a little while. She nibbled round a corner of toast as she answered his questions as to what she had planned for the day.

'After I've had my stitches out and filled in an application for a job, I thought I'd go and do a little window-shopping, since I'll have Jana's car for the afternoon,' she said carelessly, finishing up the last of her toast, and brushing her gown to get rid of the crumbs. 'Window-shopping is about all I can afford!' With this she turned a smiling face to him and found him frowning. Her smile began to fade. 'What is it?'

He glanced quickly at her from a heavy-looking brow. 'Nothing,' was his absent reply. Then, 'How would you like to come and see where I work, instead?'

She blinked. 'That would be nice,' she replied, surprised at the unexpected offer. 'But I don't think so, thank you all the same. I'll just run around a little bit.'

'Think you'd be bored with all my office work?' he asked lightly, but with a queer look that had her staring at him in puzzlement.

'Of course not,' she said. 'But you won't convince me that you haven't better things to do than to entertain an impromptu guest. Maybe some time when you know I'm coming and have planned for the visit would be better for you.'

'I think,' he said drily, 'that I might be a tolerable judge of my own affairs, thank you.' His expression was unreadable, and to her eyes, formidable.

At this she started to feel a little angry. 'If you're going to be like this all day, I'm not sure that I want to visit you,' she remarked with a tinge of acid. 'I was only trying to be polite, you know. There's no need for you to feel that you have to entertain me. I'm perfectly able to enjoy an afternoon by myself.'

He sighed. 'Just so. My fault for not using a little

more tact. Of course you need some time by yourself.'
The way he put that last remark made it sound as if he
fully expected that the reason she'd refused was
because she did not want to be with him.

'Of course I don't need time by myself!' she
snapped, confounded. 'I've had time to myself for the
past seven days! I just want to get out for a while.'

'Do you think,' he said conversationally, 'that you
might invite Marian to go with you? Poor thing, it
would do her good to get out and shop. She doesn't
manage to get out enough.'

'What I think is,' she uttered with an awful calm,
'that you'd better tell me just why you're acting so
strangely. Why, in heaven's name, don't you want me
out by myself?'

Luke drained his mug and set it on the tray with
a solid bump. Then he turned to look at her fully,
and his expression was so forbidding that she
instinctively moved back from him. In a stern and
uncompromising voice, he stated, 'I didn't want to
tell you, Kate, but you leave me no choice. I think
we were followed last night. I think you are being
watched. I believe the fellow you described last
night is the one that is watching you.' Her face
started to whiten at his words: for the past seven
days she had felt like she'd started a whole new life,
and to be reminded of the unpleasant events was
enough to send her old fears back. 'I believe that he
is hired by your father.' His voice softened as he
beheld her distress. 'Kate, I don't want you by
yourself in public, and I didn't want to tell you
about it. I'm worried about you, love.'

The happy glow that had been so evident in her eyes
last night, this morning, indeed, for the past several
days, died. Her eyes were full of that curious hardness
that seemed to darken them and make her un-

approachable. Her face was shuttered, as it had been when he had first met her.

He made a quick gesture towards her and then his hand dropped. 'Don't look like that, Kate. Don't act that way. I wish I hadn't told you.' His head bowed and he watched the circles that his left forefinger was drawing in front of him on the sheet. It would go first left, counter-clockwise twice, and then right in a clockwise direction once. He repeated this pattern over and over again. Eyes drawn to this, she then looked up into his face. He seemed tired suddenly, and the lines beside his firm mouth were pronounced, the curve to his lips unhappy.

'How easy,' she said, 'it is to let down one's guard! I'd really convinced myself that things were changed, but they're not quite, are they? I'd only thought they were. Oh, don't look at me like that, as if I'm somebody else! You see, I'm not. I'm still me. I've done a lot of growing and changing in the past several days. I think when you reach a change in perspective it's impossible to go back to what you were before.' Her green eyes were steadily regarding him, and there crept back into her gaze what soon appeared to be a smile. 'James could only hurt me emotionally when I let him, and I will never let him again. But I'd forgotten, you see, that there are other ways of hurting a person. I'd grown lax. I should have realised it last night when I had thought that the man was familiar, but I didn't. Now it seems like the memory of where I'd seen him is just around a corner of my mind, and if I hurry fast enough, I'll catch up with it before it whisks out of sight again. It'll come to me sooner or later. I owe you a great deal, Luke. Don't berate yourself for having told me the truth! You were fulfilling a promise you made me. You've done me a great service by letting me know, and I'm not upset—

at least not the way you think. I'm upset with myself
for having forgotten so easily the lesson of a lifetime:
namely, never, ever turn my back on my father's
vindictive spitefulness.

'I'll leave now and let you get dressed. Maybe I'll go
back to bed, since I am a little tired. And I'll get
Marian to come with me this afternoon. I promise
you, I won't be alone and in a vulnerable position.
And I swear to you this; I will not forget again.'

That night, she asked Jana as the four sat down to a
rather quickly prepared supper how long it would be
before she heard if she had got the job or not. 'I really
don't have much of an idea,' Jana told her. 'However,
it should be soon, I would think, since it does take a
few weeks to train the aides, and they are wanting the
addition to the staff immediately. Don't fret, my dear.
I'm sure you'll hear one way or another by the end of
next week.'

She was right; the next Wednesday showed
Katherine dancing down the hall after a phone call,
and she sang, 'I got it! I got it! I go-o-ot it!' Bursting
into the kitchen, she was regarded by several pairs of
interested and puzzled eyes, a few of which belonged
to little creatures which padded over to sniff
speculatively at her stockinged feet. She beamed at the
two women sitting at the table and told them
impressively, 'They were extremely pleased with my
appearance at the interview at the beginning of this
week, and would be happy to welcome me to the staff
at Memorial—and training begins next Tuesday! Isn't
that just fabulous?' She threw her arms about herself
in ecstasy, and laughed.

'But my dear,' replied Jana mildly. 'I didn't expect
anything else.'

'Oh, stuff! Just because you pulled a few strings for

me——' she began, but was interrupted by a delighted chuckle.

'Love, they never even called me. You got that job by yourself.'

She stared. 'Well! In that case, I think I'll go and call Luke.' She beamed at them once more quite blindingly, and sped on down the hall, leaving the two ladies to look at each other with a laughing indulgence. Katherine in the meantime picked up the phone in the hall and dialled the number to Luke's office. The ringing was answered by a cool, detached and sterile voice inquiring politely the business of the caller. 'Could you let me talk to Luke Dalton, please?' Katherine asked, as politely as the other woman. She was answered with a definite negative, and asked if she would like to schedule an appointment for the next week to see him, to which she replied, 'Nuts. I live with him and will see him tonight, but this is urgent. Tell him it's Katherine.' The disembodied voice, sounding a little shaken, asked her to hold. In a moment she heard a click.

'Kate?', it was Luke's voice, and he sounded quite rough. 'What's wrong? Is someone hurt?'

'Why,' she enquired, 'would you think that anyone had been hurt? That secretary of yours is quite off-putting, you see. Oh, Luke, do you know what?'

In comparison to his first explosive enquiry, his voice sounded astonishingly mild. 'Not personally, but if you hum a few bars . . .? You had mentioned that it was urgent, but forget that, I quite understand that you wanted to get past my secretary, although what you said to shake her up so, I can't imagine.'

She said, amused, 'I just told her that I lived with you, that's all.' At the explosive snort of laughter, she too chuckled. 'It did seem to send her off her stride a bit. I hope you don't mind?'

'Mind? I'm positively enchanted. What was it you're panting to tell me? I'm very intrigued.'

'I got it! The job, I mean. The hospital just called to tell me,' she bubbled. 'Isn't that just the most fantastic news you've ever heard? I just can't believe it! Of course it's only part time, but the pay will be nice. Actually it's not much at all, but it'll be the first paying job I'll have ever had! Heavens, I feel almost sick from excitement, and Jana says that I got it entirely on my own—isn't that great?'

'I find myself overwhelmed,' he murmured in response. 'So we have cause to celebrate tonight?'

'You bet! Maybe I'll fix us an extra special dessert as a treat. You know what I'll probably do,' she said, suddenly struck with an unappealing idea. 'I'll probably be so nervous that I'll end up going home sick to my stomach on the very first day.' This too was accompanied by a mirthful snort. 'You think I'm acting stupidly, don't you? I am, too. This can't be so interesting to you, I'll bet. You're so—so experienced that you're laughing at how I'm acting, aren't you?'

'Whoa! Back off, little dragon! I completely understand,' he exclaimed, although still with the laughter in his voice. 'I felt the exact same way when I got my first job—I'm sure that everyone does. But I can't help laughing at you. You know you're being amusing.'

'Well,' she retorted, grinning at the brown panelling in front of her. 'Don't you think I've reason to be happy? Look, I know you're probably in conference, or something vastly important, so I'll see you tonight, all right?'

'Even if I was in conference, I'd still want to hear from you. You seem to have my secretary trained correctly, so feel free to call any time. See you.'

He walked through the front door early, and at the

sound of the door slamming shut, several heads from various doors popped out. 'Early, love?' inquired Jana with obvious absent-mindedness, as she was engrossed in a particularly exciting scene in a thriller. Her head soon disappeared.

'Dinner's going to be late,' announced Marian, from the opening to the kitchen. 'Matilda ate some of the chicken before we caught her, and so we're thawing more meat.' Her head too disappeared. It was Katherine, and the guilty Matilda perched in her arms looking particularly well fed, who came forward to greet him with a pleased smile of surprise on her face. The cat looked indifferent.

'What a treat! I'm glad you're home early, but how did you manage that? Matty the Monster didn't get the dessert. I had put it away before she explored the counter. What are you hiding behind your back?—oh! Flowers, for me?' She held out a hand, immensely pleased. Somehow, Luke ended up holding a patently uninterested cat after he had passed the flowers on to Katherine. He put Matty down, and she slipped quickly down the hall, like a slinky shadow. As Katherine opened the covered package, her eyes grew soft and round and her smile became radiant. 'I adore roses. These are so beautiful!' She turned her glowing gaze at him and found him watching her with a soft and smiling expression, reminding her of his unguarded, open look when he first opened his eyes from sleep to see her by his bed. She impulsively reached up and kissed him on the mouth, backed away, and laughed into his eyes.

'This is an occasion to celebrate, isn't it?' he asked her, twitching the end of her nose in a way that had her swatting him away.

'Yes, but don't get fresh,' she said haughtily in a way that had him hooting at her in derision. 'Let me go and put these in water. I'll pour us a drink afterwards, if you like.'

'That sounds nice. I'm going to go upstairs and change in the meantime. What were we going to have for dinner, by the way?'

'Barbecued chicken,' she laughed. 'Matty got to the meat as it was thawing. Now I think we are having barbecued ribs.' As Luke started up the stairs, she hurried into the kitchen to find a vase and filled it with water and roses, later carrying it into the library to set on the table nearest the rocking-chair. Jana was roused from her absorption in her novel to exclaim over the beautiful buds. Soon Luke strolled into the room.

'Why, dear, how positively satanic!' Jana said happily at the sight of his black slacks and rolled-neck black sweater. He did look striking, and Katherine gazed at him in admiration also. His glossy hair was very slightly ruffled, and although he was in an easy pose of complete relaxation, she knew that he was capable of a dangerous attitude.

He was inspecting the title of Jana's paperback with a grimace. 'Now, I suppose you'll be imagining me as the villain of the piece for your own amusement,' he commented drily as he handed her back the book. 'How you can immerse yourself so totally and enthusiastically in one of those things, I'll never know.'

'But it's so diverting to see you as a devil,' she gurgled. 'You were such a wild thing when you were small! But I must say, you've become absolutely prosaic in your middle age!' Her young-looking blue eyes sparkled up at him.

'If I'm in my middle age,' he enquired silkily, 'where exactly are you, my love? Katie, you promised me a drink.'

She jumped up from her curled-up position in the

rocking-chair where she'd been watching the exchange between siblings with the greatest enjoyment. 'So I did, and I forgot, you poor, parched thing. Sit down, sit down,' she murmured, leading him to a chair and solicitously providing him with a pillow. 'You're too old to be always exerting yourself like this—ouch! Stop hitting me with that pillow! All right, I'm going, so stop it, will you?' Under fire, she ran from the room, only to stick her head back a moment later to observe him with dancing eyes. 'Warm milk?' she asked him, with a nice show of concern. He launched out of his chair, and she shrieked as he chased her all the way to the kitchen.

At the end of a very pleasant evening, interspersed with bouts of hilarity prompted alternately by the antics of the puppy and the three cats, Marian's too-dignified pose, and Jana's unique views (mainly, cheating outrageously) on the playing of various table games, all lounged in the library before going up to bed. They were for the most part silent and contemplative, each thinking pleasant thoughts and unwilling for the evening to end.

Jana stirred after a bit and her kindly gaze turned to Katherine who was stretched out flat on the huge leather couch. 'You've had the chance now to get to know us, Katherine,' she said: 'How do you like living here? Are you comfortable?'

She turned her golden, shiny head to look into the questioning eyes of Luke, seated across from her. 'I am constantly surprised,' she said softly. 'Every day spent here is good, every evening fun. I find I *want* to stay home all the time, and get out only as a pleasant diversion instead of as a needed escape. You see? I automatically called this household "home". It's wonderful here. And yet, I keep feeling,' she continued reflectively, turning her head away to look at the fine, expensive leather on her other side, 'an obscure fear that this won't last, that it's all an illusion, and that everything will all disappear in the night, and I'll wake up the next morning in my bed at my father's house. It will all have been a pleasant dream that will fade away before I fully recall it.'

'It won't fade,' Luke said. His voice seemed to bring her back out of the rather frightening flight of fantasy that she had been trapped in. It was a strong and reassuring statement because it was said with strength and conviction. 'It will never fade, Kate. This is reality, this is the true existence, not that shallow mimicry that you knew before. This is where you find a real strength and happiness. You've experienced life as it should be, my dear. You've only had a little taste of what is to come.'

CHAPTER EIGHT

LUKE was quite right; in the ensuing weeks, Katherine felt herself blossoming into a greater happiness than she had ever known before. It showed in her light, springy step, and her twinkling eyes. She found each morning a delight, and looked forward to the future in a way that previously she would have deemed impossible. At first she felt positively giddy, and to the bemusement of the rest of the household, came and went like a veritable whirlwind. But soon her high spirits were calming into a gentle and becoming dignity, and an unselfish kindness.

Her job was a steadying influence on her. On the first day, she came away from the hospital under absolutely no illusions as to just how subordinate her position was. On the second day, usually unflappably calm, she was very nearly reduced to tears at strict admonishments from the head nurse on the ward where she had been assigned. On the third day her patience was severely tried by the crotchetiness of an irascible old man that she was supposed to help feed. The encounter ended up with her roundly telling the old fellow off as she dripped with the lukewarm soup he had thrown at her, and the head nurse clucked about in an effort to restore order and the good humour of both parties.

She was working part time, afternoons during the week and evenings at the weekend, which left only the evenings during the week and the early part of the day at the weekend when she could see Luke. This was a bit frustrating for her, but as he never expressed any other sentiment than approval for her job, she concealed her emotions as best she could.

This was hard for one of the things that had grown in the several weeks was their relationship. They had developed an intimacy and a close understanding that was, she thought, quite special. She felt more at ease with him than she did with anyone else, and suspected that he felt the same about her. Many times, each would know what the other was thinking without a word being said aloud. It was a measure of how well they understood one another. He was her confidant, her guide, her loyal and sympathetic friend. Gradually the awareness grew on her that he was also her love.

It did not come to her in a blinding flash, or a blaze of passion. It crept up on her, catching her unawares one rainy evening as they sat together in silence. He had a book in his hands and was concentrating on it, his dark hair falling over his brow and the lean, sinewy hands holding the chunky hardback as if it were a small paperback. She had a book in her own hands, but was not attending to it. Instead she was inspecting every line and mark on Luke's lean face. Her eyes traced the slight shadows of weariness under his eyes and took in the stubble of beard that was characteristic of the end of the day. The knowledge came upon her then, like a gentle and easy sigh breathed at a whiff of an elusive, fragrant summer's breeze. Only instead of passing away with barely a conscious thought, this stayed with her and grew stronger with each passing day.

In a way, the knowledge was the cause of a greater ease she experienced when she was near him. Although she was not exactly sure how he felt about her, she was sure of how she felt about him. She no longer had to wonder at how her pulse would race from a casual kiss on the cheek, or an arm about her shoulders. It was a measure of the trust she felt for him, this easiness of attitude. Luke would never, she knew, consciously hurt her.

She kept her promise to him and never went out in public alone. This was easy for Jana drove her to work in the afternoons when she put in her own volunteer work, and Luke picked her up either on his way home from work during the week, or making a special trip for her in the evenings at the weekend. When she had offered to pay for the petrol used on these special trips, he had absolutely refused.

'You nut,' was his reply. 'I *want* to do it, so keep your blasted money, will you?' This inelegant and ungentle speech had her in quite a glow.

One fine August morning, Katherine went bouncing around the house, knocking on closed bedroom doors and calling gaily for everyone to wake up. She heard a groan from behind Jana's door. Marian didn't answer at all, and she opened the door to tell her that she most absolutely emphatically should get up, to which that lady's only reaction was to hide her head underneath the pillow. Knocking on Luke's door, she shouted to him to get up quickly and was rewarded with the sight of him pulling open his door very fast, surprising her with the unexpectedness of it.

His hair was rumpled and his body encased in his blue dressing-gown, but his face was quite alert and his eyes clear. 'What is the reason for all this racket?' was his mild enquiry.

She grinned at him impishly. 'Come downstairs and find out!' she told him and whisked away before he could reply. Another knock at Jana's door had her peeking around it and blinking sleepily.

'I don't show my face before eight,' she said decisively and slowly smiled at Katherine's obvious high spirits.

'You've got to come down this morning,' Katherine told her. 'You just have to. Otherwise you'll miss the whole thing.' She started to skip down the stairs, leaving Jana sufficiently intrigued to wrap her dressing-gown about her and join Luke and Marian in the hall to follow after.

A marvellous sight greeted their eyes when they reached the kitchen. The table was set very prettily, with a few fresh flowers in a bouquet as the centrepiece, and the best china was laid out for four on a freshly ironed tablecloth. By each setting was a pretty bowl of freshly cut fruit. Coffee steaming in mugs was set with precision just to the right of the plates. A huge, covered platter was in the middle of the table with a jug of what turned out to be warm syrup and a pot of honey in attendance nearby. Orange juice was poured, and bacon was seen to be sizzling on the stove. There were three little wrapped packages by three plates.

'Oh my,' murmured Marian, overcome. She sank into a chair weakly and was told by Katherine that she would have to move since that was Jana's place. To this statement, she started up and sat where she was directed.

'This is quite too much,' Jana said, looking about at the splendid sight with awe. 'It's so early—how early did you have to get up, to fix all this?'

Luke was regarding Katherine's amused face thoughtfully, as he sat in the spot designated for him. She uncovered the platter to reveal golden brown pancakes that smelt delicious, and the four helped themselves with a will. 'What's the occasion, love?' he asked curiously.

She wrinkled her nose at him. 'Not now,' she admonished him through a mouthful of bacon. 'Everyone can eat first, and then we'll open presents!' She was the only one fully dressed, in faded jeans that had flour down the legs, and a sweater. Her hair was pulled back in a saucy pony-tail, making her look like a teenager.

Jana, looking around, observed little packages wrapped and sitting by the animals' cardboard bed, and pointed this fact out to the other two.

'This is nutty,' said Marian, shaking her frizzled head. 'But I like it.' The pancakes were fluffy and light, quite perfect, and Katherine had the satisfaction of seeing all tuck into her surprise with flattering enthusiasm.

When everyone had at last finished their huge repast and sat back from their empty plates, she got up and removed the plates and filled up the cups again with fresh coffee. Then, sitting down and pouring cream into her own cup, she grinned delightedly at the three pairs of eyes that were regarding her, a question in Jana's and Marian's and a definite twinkle of amusement in Luke's. 'Open your presents!' she urged each. 'Go on, I want to see you!'

With her urging, they each picked up the wrapped packages and started to unwrap them; Jana did so with a painstaking care as she picked delicately at each piece of tape, Marian with a ripping gusto, and Luke with several questioning, smiling glances at Katherine, who was seated opposite him. The unveiling of the gifts showed an exclusive French perfume spray for Jana, a new hardback book that she had known that Marian especially wanted, and a pewter unicorn statue for Luke. The two women exclaimed with delight over their gifts, but she was looking at Luke as he placed the delicately featured little statue with exquisite care on the table. His face held an odd expression, as if he was quite struck with it, and under cover of the two women's chatter to each other, she asked him, 'Do you know what the unicorn symbolises?'

He watched her as if he couldn't take his eyes away. 'Tell me,' he said quietly.

Her eyes smiled at him. 'It usually signifies purity, but it can also symbolise happiness, and that is what I mean this statue to say to you.'

He reached out a gentle finger, looking quite touched, and traced the slight point of the graceful horse's horn down the neck to the curve of the back. 'A gift of happiness,' he murmured, a strange, sweet smile on his softened face.

His eyes once again lifted to her, and they held an emotion that she suddenly dared not read for fear that she would misunderstand, and she dropped her own. She whispered, 'Thank you, Luke, for everything you've done for me.'

Jana caught this last remark and asked her, 'Is it a "thank you" to all of us that you meant with these gifts?'

Her eyes turned to Jana's and suddenly she was brimming over again with that slightly mischievous good spirit that had been evident earlier. 'Oh, no,' she gurgled, wrapping her arms about herself with glee. Everyone blinked at each other in puzzlement, and she sang out suddenly, 'Happy birthday to me, happy birthday to me! Happy birthday, dear me-e ...' and she ruined the whole song by pealing off into a fit of laughter at the looks of astonishment and dismay on everyone's face.

After the first upshoot of his eyebrows, Luke appeared to be very amused, but Jana and Marian were quite horrified. 'Why, this is terrible!' Jana gasped, looking at her with an expression of stupefaction.

Marian said sternly, 'You should have had breakfast made for you, instead of you making breakfast for everyone else! And as for you buying presents for us—don't you know, you mixed-up child, that *you're* the one that's supposed to get presents today?'

Katherine showed her a crestfallen face. 'Don't you like your present?' she asked in such piteous tones that Luke had to cover up his face.

At this reaction from her admonishment, Marian looked even more horrified. 'Of course I do! But you still shouldn't have done it, you know. Why, it's ridiculous to think of it.'

'Oh then, by all means, let's think of it!' she replied, abandoning her act and leaning back with a smile. 'Just why do you think I did such a thing?'

The question had the two women sitting back too, with attitudes of confoundment. Luke looked from his sister to Marian, gauging their thoughts and smiling. 'Well, you obviously see it as a special occasion,' said Jana, 'which of course it is, but you didn't react with any embarrassment or disclaimers like most people do on their birthdays.'

'Exactly,' she nodded in affirmation. She stood and waved away all helping hands as she stacked the last of the dishes from breakfast and carried them to the sink. 'You see,' she threw over her shoulder, 'I just wanted to share.'

Katherine had cause for a good deal of amusement during the day after Luke had left. Whenever she entered the room, Jana and Marian would fall silent and look like two pictures of innocence. Of course she knew what they were planning, and it quite delighted her to see their rather obvious conspiracy.

She was on the kerb outside the hospital at the prescribed time after work and readily hopped into the Ferrari when Luke swept up. He spared her a quick flash of his teeth before shooting away from the kerb and pulling into the thick stream of traffic. 'Had a good day?' he asked her.

'No better than some, and a lot worse than others,' she laughed. 'No, really, I had a pretty normal day, considering.'

It wasn't long before they pulled into the driveway. He stopped to let her out before putting the car away, and she paused for a minute with her hand on the door handle, looking at him mischievously. 'Should I pretend to be surprised?' she asked him, which had his shoulders shaking.

'That might be a bit much,' he told her. 'Just act gratified. That should work in any situation.'

She wrinkled her nose at him impudently and whisked out of the car to spring up the steps. As no one was near the front door, she was able to slip up to her room unnoticed and change out of her uniform in peace. However, when she got downstairs again, Marian cornered her in the hall and firmly shepherded her into the library and ordered her to stay there until otherwise notified. Since she had left her book resting on the side table by the couch and there was a thoughtfully placed glass of wine waiting on the coffee table, she complied and was soon joined by Luke. He was also out of his working suit and he reclined next to her on the couch with a shot of whisky, which she eyed with distaste. He caught her look.

'What? Don't tell me you have objections to my whisky!' was his wicked response. She sipped her glass and raised a silent, inquisitive eyebrow. 'The first time I saw you, you were tossing off a shot with the most admirable and experienced aplomb! I was most impressed, I must confess, to see you swallow it all in one go without choking! Not everyone can do that, didn't you know? Are you going to tell me that it was all an act?'

'Every inch of it, my good man,' she replied. 'I

absolutely abhor whisky. In fact, I'd never had a shot before that night. It was as detestable as I'd expected.'

'Good heavens!' he exclaimed, a delighted smile hovering on his firm lips. 'And you took it like a trooper. Whatever possessed you to do such a thing?'

'My father,' she said gently, 'hated to see me drink hard liquor at his parties. Bad for image.'

'Provoking puss,' he said, sipping at his glass with evident enjoyment, at which she shuddered.

Jana stuck her head in the door, said, 'Dinner,' and disappeared again. They looked at each other contemplatively.

'I believe,' she said with a show of dismay, 'that it is about to start?' She stood with him and turned to the door.

'Take it,' he whispered wickedly, 'like a trooper.' She decided to ignore this and sailed into the dining-room.

She was not disappointed. The table was set very attractively, and beside one plate, there were three wrapped packages. This made her smile, but what really made her laugh was Marian's disgusted comment, 'You spoiled the whole thing, you know, when you did the same thing for breakfast!'

She sat down where the presents were, and did a credible job of ignoring them as they ate her favourite meal of lamb shish kebabs with broccoli and cheese sauce, and crescent rolls. The meal was followed not by a cake, which she had half expected, but a laden plate of chocolate chip cookies with plenty of pecans, one of her more disastrous weaknesses. She moaned as she saw the huge plate presented to her. 'I bet you made a double batch, too,' she uttered with such despair that everyone laughed. A previous batch, now consigned to history, had mysteriously been sampled at unknown times, and had disappeared at a record rate. Everyone had denied knowledge, except Katherine, who had been bright pink with guilt.

Despite her moan, she dug into the cookies with an enthusiasm that had Marian and Jana smiling at each other, and munched through several before turning to the presents with an air of eagerness that had Luke smiling. The first present she opened was from Jana, and it was wrapped in a pretty shade of pale blue. It turned out to be two delicately carved wooden hair combs that were dyed a deep burgundy. She exclaimed with delight over them; they were a perfect shade for her hair. Marian's present to her was a pair of slim leather gloves. When she turned her grateful gaze to Marian, that lady said, 'After all, it is August, and autumn is just around the bend, you know, and you don't have a thing for the cold weather.'

She turned to her present from Luke last. She'd saved it, because she knew that no matter what he gave her, she would cherish it more than anything she received from anyone else. It was a very small box, wrapped plainly. In fact, it was so small that she knew it must be jewellery, and was suddenly afraid to open it and see what was inside. Her eyes lifted to him. He was, for a change, not smiling at all now, and his eyes seemed to hold some sort of message that she was not quite able to read. He seemed tense, but appeared to relax when her eyes silently questioned him, and he nodded for her to go ahead and open the package.

She tore off the paper, finding a little black velvet box and her hands inexplicably trembling. She stared down at its square shape for a long moment, and looked into Luke's dark eyes. At this, he did smile faintly, and this gave her the courage to open the small box. What she saw made her turn so pale that Jana uttered an exclamation of alarm. Then, a lovely tide of colour washed over her, and she raised huge, brimming eyes to stare in Luke's direction and nod. His chair scraped, and she barely had enough time to put down the little box before she was caught up into his arms and held very tightly. The tears spilled over, and he tilted her face up to wipe away each one with a tender finger, murmuring softly. Then with an exquisite gentleness, he bent his head to hers, and Jana and Marian were forgotten.

Feeling overcome, Marian reached over to pick up the little box and peer into it. She turned the box to Jana. Nestled into the rich black velvet winked a marvellous blue solitaire diamond in yellow gold. The two ladies looked at each other and at the pair who were so close. Without a word, and by mutual consent, they rose from the table and tiptoed away.

After a time, Luke raised his head, and he looked down into her face. Her hair was tousled about her face from his caressing fingers, and her cheeks were quite flushed. Her eyes held a shimmery, rather unfocused glow, and her lips looked very kissed. She was, he told her, quite beautiful. 'Are you sure?' he asked, tracing the edge of her lower lip with one finger. It trembled and she nodded silently, not trusting her voice to speech just yet. He reached behind him to pick up the box, extracting the ring from it and holding up her hand. He slipped it on her left ring finger. She was immeasurably surprised to find it fitted.

'How in the world did you manage that?' she asked him in astonishment. His smile was almost unbearably sweet.

'Marian knew your glove size from the rubber gloves you wear when you're helping in the kitchen,' he told her. 'That was how, she told me, that she was going to get your size for the leather gloves. I stole the trick from her, and hoped it would fit.' He looked deeply into her eyes, and very seriously. 'I love you, Kate,' he said. 'I love you so much. I think I did when you walked into the room at that party. It's just that I didn't realise until later.'

She put her hand up to his cheek. It was impossible, she thought dazedly, to feel any more happiness that this. It was impossible to feel any more love. 'When did you first decide that you did love me?' she asked quietly. He turned his dark head and kissed her hand before replying.

'I think it really hit me the first day you were here, when you cried so, and I held you on my lap in the kitchen,' he said tenderly, touching her nose with his mouth lightly. 'All I could think of was how much I'd give just to see you happy and smiling. My feelings were so intense and jolted me so hard, that when I went to work I was considerably shaken. I didn't get a thing done all day, and all I could think about was getting home to see if you were all right. I did ring that day, but you were sleeping, and I asked Jana not to tell you I'd rung. You were so vulnerable! I wanted to protect you from ever being hurt again. I always want to see you smiling.' His lips came down on hers in a feathery kiss.

Her arms had slid up around his neck as he had talked, and she now responded to his kiss gladly, deepening it of her own accord. He broke it off with a wrench. 'Ah, let's talk, shall we?' he asked her, his voice sounding a little rough. She put her head down on his shoulder, snuggled deep into his welcoming arms, and nodded happily. She was considerably surprised when he put her away from him. '*No*, Kate. You sit there, and I'll sit right here. There, now why don't you tell me when you first knew?'

She reached across the table and his hand instantly

closed over hers, giving her a little thrill. 'I can't say for sure,' she murmured, her eyes going dreamy with remembrance. 'All I can say is that one night you were sitting and reading, and I was rocking in the rocking-chair, and I looked into your tired face and thought to myself, "I love him." It was as simple as that, and yet a very profound moment—oh, I can't explain myself very well. I just knew one night, that's all.'

He brought her hand to his lips. 'That's enough, my love. Believe me, that is quite enough.'

After talking for some time in low voices, they moved to the library to sit close together on the couch. She snuggled up to him, with her head on his shoulder and her body curved into his own position. They did talk a little more, but mostly spent the time just being together. She fell asleep on his shoulder.

The sensation, she thought dreamily, was a familiar one. Where had she felt it before? Her eyes flew open: her head was on Luke's shoulder, and he was carrying her up the stairs. 'Mmm,' was her contented response as she buried her head into his warm neck. 'But I really can walk up myself.'

'I know,' he whispered, tightening his arms. 'But I want to carry you.' And so he did.

'But,' she protested sleepily, 'I don't want to go to bed yet, Luke. Let's stay downstairs for a little longer.'

'It's very late,' he said to her softly, as he deposited her just outside her door. 'And even if you can sleep in the morning, I have an early appointment. Besides, everyone else is in bed. Jana popped in while you were asleep and told me she was going up some time ago.'

'I was not,' she mumbled, unable to resist the urge to rub at her eyes, 'asleep.'

'Oh, I see,' was his response. 'Did you remember Jana coming into the room a while ago?'

'Er, no,' she sheepishly replied. 'But that doesn't mean anything.'

'Ah!' he said, with air of the greatest comprehension. 'I understand now! You were resting your eyes and thinking very hard!'

'Yes, I was!' she stuck to her story in spite of the twinkle in Luke's eyes. Then, she looked back at him with something like fear in hers. 'Luke, I—I don't want it to end.'

His face gentled unbelievably. 'It won't, love,' he whispered, and touched her lips with his own. 'I swear to you that. It won't.' Then, without waiting to see if she went straight inside or not, he turned and strode on down to his room, shutting the door behind him.

It was incredible, she thought sleepily as she opened her eyes the next morning and looked at the brilliant ring on her left hand, how good life can be. She knew a sudden fear; life was, she felt, too good. How unreal events seemed in comparison to how her life had been such a short time ago! Something would happen, and her whole world would come crashing down around her ears. What, she couldn't say, but something would happen.

She was still huddled under the covers and thinking unpleasant thoughts when Jana knocked on her door. 'Come in,' she called, sitting up quickly.

The door opened and Jana slipped in, carrying a hot steaming mug and wearing a delightful smile. 'Now I'm pulling a Katherine trick,' she announced with a twinkle. 'Here, dear. I'm so happy for you.'

'You are? I find I'm very happy, too!' Katherine twinkled back. She stretched out lazily. 'Oh, Jana! Life isn't supposed to be this good to me. I—I don't trust it, when it hands me someone so incredibly wonderful, like Luke. It's all going to blow away at the first strong wind, and . . .' Her eyes met the older woman's and saw the kindness in those blue eyes. 'I'm being stupid. I think I'd better get dressed, don't you?' She kicked off the covers and got up.

Contrary to her rather unformed fears, nothing in the next few days proclaimed disaster. In fact, she felt as if she were floating through a fairy tale, she was so supremely happy.

She loved her new appointment on the children's ward, and was soon a favourite with both nurses and patients. Of course, many were too sick to be very aware of anything outside their own discomfort, but the ones who could enjoyed her careful attention. She found to her own surprise that she possessed an abundance of patience with the little ones, more so than with the older folks. Soon she was the one called upon to help feed Susie, who wouldn't let anyone else feed her, or to calm little Joseph when his mother left to eat supper. They were, she told Luke, much better behaved than the older folks.

This pattern of serenity lasted for several days.

The hospital was being operated with a skeleton staff, because of an outbreak of 'flu, and both Katherine and Jana were putting in extra hours. One afternoon, Jana called Luke's office and told him not to come and pick up Katherine. 'We've had a bit of an upset,' she told him, a note of strain underlying her calm voice, 'and quite a few are staying over their shifts. There's been a street fight and several bystanders were seriously hurt. A car swerved to miss a little boy who was mistakenly pushed out into the street, and caused a three-car accident, so things are going to be a mess. We should be getting the first ambulance in a few minutes—what a time to be short-staffed! See you later.'

In the meantime, Katherine was involved in a very personal crisis of her own.

CHAPTER NINE

THE front door opened with a crash, and Katherine walked in quickly, checking only at the sight of Luke coming down the hall. They looked at each other for a moment, his shocked ejaculation bursting forth at the sight of her reddened dress, and her white, set face with the blazing green eyes. She broke away from his gaze, feeling a little odd as the world seemed to blur a bit, but then she focused on the stairs. She started up them very fast. He was quick behind her, even quicker than Jana, who had come in at the door just behind Katherine.

'Kate—Kate!' he called after her sharply, but she made no reply. She entered her room with the same sort of crash that had heralded her entrance to the house and strode across to the bathroom, slamming the door and locking it behind her. Luke was only a mere split second behind her, but it was long enough for her to barricade herself in. He pounded on the door after her. 'Kate! Let me in, love. Come on, let me in!'

There was no answer. Katherine had listened for a moment to his voice as she leaned against the locked door, and she felt the door heave with his pounding. She couldn't seem to feel anything, though. She didn't feel the slightest inclination to open the door as he'd asked her to. She hadn't felt anything after that knife-like pain when the little boy had died beneath her fingertips. She couldn't even remember how she had got into her bathroom, but that didn't matter. She was glad, because she didn't want to feel anything, not ever again.

If life could be cruel to her, she thought tiredly, resting her head against the vibrating door, then it had been unbearably cruel to that little boy. A deep, agonised sob broke from her as she began to experience again that knife-like pain.

She had been mercifully numb as the head nurse had pulled her away from the little body, and she had continued feeling that dull, sustaining numbness as Jana, told of what had happened, later drove her home. She had sat in uncommunicative silence all the way home, unaware and uncaring about the silent, concerned presence beside her. But now, she wasn't to have that escape.

She looked down at herself and was shocked anew at the amount of blood that had somehow got all over her. She'd been wiped off at the site, and when she had got back to the hospital she'd washed completely clean, but there was still that horrifying red down her front. A feeling of panic invaded her; she must get it all off. Scrabbling at her shoes and getting them off her feet, she started the shower going with very hot water and stepped in, clothes and all. Standing under the burning spray, she tried to erase from her mind what had happened, but she couldn't. Passing her arms round her waist tightly as she felt that knife of anguish, she cried aloud from the pain of it, and bent over double in the shower, going to her knees.

It was at that sound, coming as it did over the water's gushing, that Luke put his shoulder to the door of the bathroom and crashed into the little cubicle.

He moved faster than Jana had ever seen him move before, and was bending over, trying to get Katherine to stand up, but she was too rigid and wrapped in her own terrible grief to attend to him, and too slippery with wetness for him to be able to grasp her with any degree of safety for lifting out. Those awful, heart-rending sobs were tearing at him. He stepped into the bath and knelt beside her, pulling her into his arms and straining her close. The scalding water still streamed on them painfully, and he reached behind with one hand to turn it off. Then he put his head down on her shoulder, hiding his face in her wet hair, rocking her back and forth.

Slowly his presence penetrated her anguish, and suddenly, convulsively, she thrust her arms about his neck in a stranglehold. She pushed her face into his warm, wet neck and cried like she had never cried before.

After urging her out of the bath, he turned to his sister and said quietly that while she helped Katherine get out of her wet clothes, he would go and change himself. After making such a decisive statement, he remained for some moments, staring at Katherine's wet, bent head, until Jana gently shooed him out. When he had closed the door of the bedroom behind him, she turned to the younger girl and found her already stripping.

Katherine's teeth had began to chatter, and her lips were blue by the time she slipped into the warm nightgown that Jana had found for her and belted her dressing-gown about her slim waist. She didn't notice Jana's worried glances at her alarming silence, nor did she feel the gentle helping fingers that prompted her to sit on the edge of the bed, and later brushed out the sodden tangles in her long hair.

Katherine had thought that she could feel no greater pain than she had already experienced. She had also thought that she could feel no greater happiness. She had been wrong on one count: the pain that she felt now, the first grief she'd experienced for a human being other than herself, was deeper than any self-absorbed emotion she'd ever known. She knew, for the first time, how deeply one can hurt for another's plight. She had tasted the consequences of a life built on caring for others.

The way she felt now, she never wanted to care for another person as long as she lived. And so it was, when Luke re-entered her room scant minutes later in dry clothes, his damp hair brushed off his forehead, that he found her completely absorbed in herself. She had retreated from the outside world to her dark, bitter thoughts. When Jana quietly talked with Luke over her head, she heard every word that was spoken; one part of her mind even registered and understood what was said. But for the most part her consciousness rejected the whole conversation and anything addressed to her as superfluous. It was, in comparison to what she was experiencing inside, unimportant.

'She hasn't spoken a word to me since you left,' Jana told him worriedly. 'In fact, she never spoke at all on the way home from the hospital. Luke, I'm very concerned about the way she's handling all this.'

He did no more than nod absently at his sister, his eyes dwelling thoughtfully on Katherine's sad face as, with her head bowed, she watched the pattern that her fingers were drawing on her dressing-gown. He asked Jana, 'Have you heard anything about dinner yet?'

She replied, 'Marian said something about it being ready—she poked her head in here a few minutes ago.'

'Why don't you go down and eat with Marian?' he suggested quietly. 'I'll tuck Kate into bed and sit with her until you're done. Then perhaps you could fix a tray and bring it up for the two of us, if you would?'

'Certainly,' was her immediate response. She glanced back down at Katherine's bent head, her eyes filled with sorrow. She said, 'I think they said that the little boy was five years old.' Katherine's head jerked at this, which both saw, and Jana's face was wet with tears as she left the room quickly.

Strong hands clasped tightly on her shoulders, startling her into looking up. She obediently obeyed the slight pressure and stood. Her eyes followed Luke's movements as he leaned to twitch the covers back and throw her pillows against the headboard. Then he turned back to her and a gentle arm about her shoulders coaxed her foreward to slip into the soft bed. Instead of pulling the covers up around her, as one part of her mind half-expected, he slid into the bed with her also, and then pulled the top quilted bed spread over them both. Bracing his broad back on the headboard behind him, he reached out and pulled her into his arms. She went willingly and settled on his chest with a slight sigh. Putting one leg up and letting her body fit into his strong curves, with one arm around his waist, she gradually began to relax from the awful tension that had gripped her since the early afternoon. He began to talk quietly, lightly, about several unimportant everyday circumstances in his workday, and at first the pain was almost unbearable to listen to his calm voice talking of such things and remember the terrible scene from earlier. But soon his droning voice had its desired effect, and she began to pay attention to some things that were being said. She even managed to smile at a mild witticism, although he couldn't see it from where he was. She began to feel the extreme exhaustion that so often accompanies strong grief, and soon she was dozing lightly, comforted by the even and untroubled rise and fall of his firm chest.

A quiet click roused her, and both she and Luke looked around as Jana came through the door with a loaded tray, Marian following close behind. As she put the laden tray beside the bed on the floor, Marian placed two glasses of wine that she had carried, on the bedside table. They only stayed long enough to look with deep anxiety at Katherine's silent head, but a slight smile and a shaking of Luke's dark head had them backing out.

When they had gone, Luke released Katherine to bend forward and inspect the contents of the tray. She settled back to watch him apathetically, and refused all offers of the delicious meal on the tray. She did, however, take the wine gladly, while Luke ate unhindered. She watched him, glad of the chance to concentrate on someone else after the self-absorption of her own depression. She smiled at his evident enthusiasm as he tucked into a very full plate, and this smile he did catch. His eyes met hers for a moment and his hand stilled, but what he saw seemed to reassure him, for he was soon finishing his meal after returning a smile. When he finished, he asked her if she had changed her mind about wanting to eat. With her negative shake of the head, he swung his legs off the bed, telling her that he would be back in a minute. He bent and picked up the tray, striding out of the door. The sound of footsteps on the stairs was soon heard, and she leaned back against the headboard with closed eyes.

He was back soon enough, carrying a book under one arm and a fresh glass of wine in the other. The wine he handed to her; the book he opened when he had settled on the bed against the headboard again and long legs stretched out crossed in front of him. Thus was the evening spent: when she had finished her second glass of wine, she snuggled deep into her pillow, under the covers, and watched his still face as he read.

When at last she was sleeping peacefully, Luke

lowered his book to watch her face with a deep frown of worry between his level brows. He eased off the bed carefully, watching to see if he disturbed her at all. She slept on, and he tenderly tucked the covers around her, as gentle as any mother with her only child, and with his closed book in hand, he walked silently out of the room, switching off the light but leaving the door to her room open as he went.

She was so very tired that at first her sleep was unbroken and deep. Gradually, though, her consciousness was disturbed with nightmare images flitting through her sleeping mind, and she began to toss about. This action was soon pronounced, the sweat breaking out on her brow, and the hands that had been restlessly moving about on the covers clenched the sheets very hard.

The blood was everywhere—no matter how she tried to stem the flow, it kept coming out. She was drenched all down her front, and her hands and arms, pushed frantically against the horrifying wound that rent Luke's chest, were stained almost black with it. She felt it pulse out, and knew that with every heartbeat he was pumping out his life right there in front of her eyes, and she was powerless to stop it. And all the while, his dark gentle eyes watched her with a smile in their depths. In a frenzy of horror and grief, she screamed at him, 'Don't die! Don't—don't die on me! Please, *don't die! Stop smiling at me, damn you!*' Impelled with a force prompted by terror, she sprang up, staring wildly into the darkness, her hands pressed over her cheeks and moving to her mouth to stifle the sounds of the sobs coming forth. She closed her eyes and bent over her knees, weeping, and then Luke crashed into the room, followed soon by Jana and Marian.

The two women crept out as Katherine blurted out

to Luke's bent head a veritable deluge of horror, grief and rage. Marian shut the door on her trembling voice just as she was attempting to tell him of the awful nightmare image, and the irrevocable stains on her arms from his life's blood whle he held her tightly.

Marian sent a troubled smile to Jana, murmuring, ' "What, will these hands ne'er be clean?" ' But when Jana asked her what she meant by what was obviously a quote, she shook her head. The two stood talking irresolutely for some time in the hall, but after a little bit the conversation lagged, and each went back to her room in silence.

After Katherine had started, it was as if she could not stop the flow of words, and it was quite some time before her anguished voice petered out into silence. His arms were holding her so tightly that she thought her ribs must crack from the strain, and the neck muscles where her hands were nestled felt rigid. But his voice, when she told him of her nightmare, was mild and flatly matter-of-fact when he said. 'But my dear, I'm not dead and I'm not even wounded. And I promise you that I'm definitely *not* smiling at any of this.'

That steadied her more than anything else he could have done, and soon she was able to lift her head up from its resting-place on his supporting shoulder, and loosen her death-hold from his neck. He loosened his hold on her also at this, and leaned back to look searchingly at her face. Her hair was all over the place, and he pushed it off her face with one hand. Her eyes were extremely large, with the dark circles under them that he had hoped never to see again. Her face was set into lines of bitterness and exhaustion, and the curve of her mouth was tense.

'How could God—if there is a God—let that little boy die like that?' she burst out, with such an expression of bitterness that his heart seemed to contract. 'I would have given my life, yes and gladly, too, to have that little boy live! I would far rather have died myself, than to watch his blood come out of him like that!'

'Don't say that!' He gripped her slender shoulders roughly. Her shocked eyes stared up at his brilliant expressive ones, until after a while his fell and his grip relaxed. 'I'm sorry. Of course you feel that way; I'm sure that I would have felt the same.' He smiled twistedly, and it tore her heart to see him look so. 'It's just that I could never give you up, so that someone else could live. It's asking too much of me.'

She raised a hand to cup his cheek. 'I know,' she whispered. 'I care about you the same way.' She paused, and then continued in a tone that conveyed how deeply the death of the little stranger had affected her. 'But if caring means feeling this terrible, wrenching agony, then I don't want to care at all. I don't want to care about anything. Luke, I don't want to feel this pain!'

The hurting cry, sounding like a plea for help, had him closing his eyes with a wince. He turned away from her, presenting to her the strong lines of his profile, and he bowed his head to look at his two clasped hands dangling between his knees. It was an attitude of such sorrow and strange helplessness that it made her want to hold him to her, to soothe away the troubled look, to ease his pain. She had time to wonder about this; Luke had always seemed to be so much in control. She had not realised just how much she looked to him for everything, until she saw him now at a loss as to what to say to her. In that one moment, she realised a sudden shift had taken place in the balance of their relationship. Before, he had been the one to give, and she did the majority of the taking.

It would never be that way again. Not after the exposure of his own vulnerability.

'I wish,' he was saying, 'that I could give you a life free of pain, Katherine.' He so very rarely called her by her full name. 'But I can't do that. I can't guarantee you that you are never going to hurt again, because if we get married, then one of us is going to experience a terrible loss. "For the rest of our lives" is a phrase that so rarely comes true. Do you see, my love?' As long as she lived, she would never forget the look on his face as he sat, unable to face her, and spoke to her thus. 'One of us is going to die before the other. And one of us is going to hurt more than they've ever hurt before. It is going to happen.

'I would give my right arm to save you grief, if I could. I wish I could give that little boy life. But I can't spare you any more than I could shield Jana. Pain and grief happen! But I can promise you one thing, Katherine.' He turned his bent head, and she saw the glitter in his dark eyes, and the intensity of his expression. 'I will promise you this: the more you feel, the more strength you are capable of attaining. The deeper the grief, the higher the joy. You can't change what you are—you are a caring and sensitive person, and always have been. That is why your father was capable of hurting you so much—because you cared. The more you care, the more you will be able to withstand. I can't stop your hurt, but maybe, just maybe, I can help you find your strength.'

Some deep part of her took in what he was trying so hard to say with a recognition and a welcoming, as if she had found the one thing that made her feel truly balanced and whole inside. She raised her eyes to him and found him regarding her with such a look of gentle concern and understanding that tears started in her eyes. He exclaimed with dismay at this, but she smiled

through her tears and said, 'No, no—it's all right!'
She stopped whatever he was going to say with one
finger. 'Really, Luke. I'm all right. I understand what
you are trying to tell me. I know what you say is right.
But,' at this her lips quivered, 'I—it's been such a
painful ... and I need to feel something good—oh,
just hold me.' She was drawn into his arms as she
whispered, 'Just hold me for a while.'

He groaned at this, and held her with such a
tenderness that she was quite overcome. She pressed
little soft kisses on the side of his neck, at which he
trembled. This had her crying in earnest, and she
tightened her arms around him to try and give him a
measure of the strength that he had given her. His
mouth came to hers and for a long, long time she
couldn't speak, nor did she want to. A warmth
began to invade her limbs. Then she noticed
something.

'Why do you have your clothes on?' she whispered
to him, after glancineg at the clock that read two a.m.
He was fully dressed.

'I stayed up and read in my room,' he answered her
softly, one hand fondling the hair that lay heavily on
her neck. 'You had kept so much of your pain in, that
I suspected something like this might happen, and
wanted to be near you when you needed me.'

She trembled, and whispered, 'Luke.' He looked at
her with dark eyes. 'I need you. Why do you have
your clothes on?'

'No,' he murmured in protest, but it was a feeble
sound, and at length he came down to her with the
same urgency that she felt. Once, when he was
shedding his clothes having just turned off the light,
he whispered, 'We shouldn't—you're too overwrought,
and I——'

'Hush,' she whispered. 'Why shouldn't we? I love

you, Luke. I love you more than anything else in the world.'

'Be sure,' he murmured. 'Be very sure.' There was no more talking, other than little whispered love words, for the rest of the night.

The next morning, Katherine came downstairs very late, and found Jana sitting at the kitchen table with an empty mug in front of her staring into space. 'Hello,' Katherine said softly, and was rewarded with a swift smile.

'Oh, my dear,' said Jana with relief, after scanning her face in concern. 'Luke told me before he left that you'd probably sleep in late, and so I resisted the temptation to peek in and check on you, but—are you really doing better? You worried Marian and me so, last night.'

'Oh, I'll be fine,' she said quietly. She poured herself a cup of coffee and took the pot over to Jana to pour her more too. Then she added cream and sat down. 'It'll take a while, I dare say, for the rather vivid memory to fade, but I'm getting over it. Luke mentioned something, and I wanted to ask you about it, if you don't mind.' She looked into the other woman's eyes. 'He mentioned you in a way that I didn't quite understand. He said something about being unable to "shield you too" and I was wondering if you could throw some light on that. Of course, if I'm prying just tell me so and I'll shut up.'

Something flickered in the older woman's eyes, and Katherine watched them fall away to look at the checkered tablecloth. Jana absently moved her mug around on the table, the veined and slender hands touching the salt and pepper shakers lightly and then moving on to fidget with something else. 'I think,' she said quietly, 'that he must have meant when my husband and little girl died, some years back.'

Katherine felt very sick, and closed her eyes at this statement. 'Oh, no,' she whispered. 'I had no idea. I'm sorry.'

'Oh, don't be, love. It was some time ago. Of course it still hurts me to think of it, but the pain is a gentle pain now, and almost like a friend to me.' The blue eyes smiled at her, as Jana looked up. 'It was very difficult for me at the time, and the only way I could have borne the pain, I think, was with Luke's help. He bore with my tears and fits of depression for so long! And it was he who pointed out to me that Mark would have wanted me to enjoy life, and not bury myself away like I had been doing. He said to me that Mark would have told me to reach out and make my happiness, either by myself or with someone new. And he was right, so I had to pull myself together and do just that!' Jana leaned back in her chair.

She continued, 'I think that you must have reminded him a little of me when you first came to live with us.' She was heartened by Katherine's reflective silence. 'You had that same stricken look in your eyes that I seem to remember in mine, and Luke was always a sucker for that look! He can't bear to see someone unhappy, you see, especially someone he cares about deeply, and he certainly has come to care very deeply for you! It's been such a pleasure to see him fall in love with you. Now, don't look surprised, Marian and I saw it coming a mile away! And very pleased we are, too. You are just the one for him.' Jana reached out and patted her arm. 'And don't you let anyone convince you differently, dear!'

Katherine had been given the day off, and so when she finally went back to work, she was able to show the usual calm, unruffled appearance that she had acquired and now displayed on the job.

Luke did not come back to her room after that one

night, saying when they had talked about it, that he had really wanted to wait until the wedding, and although he couldn't regret the night under the circumstances, he would be hesitant to repeat it. 'We have to think of Marian and Jana,' he said gently, in response to her baffled enquiry. 'Much as I want to, love, I'd rather not hurt either, and I'm not sure how they'd react.' She thought she understood after that, but in the ensuing days, she detected a certain, inexplicable reserve in Luke's attitude towards her. She found it strangely hard to manoeuvre things so that she could spend time alone with him, and she caught odd, unsmiling glances from him when he thought she wasn't looking. This observation puzzled her, and concerned her a little, but since they had set a date for the wedding in a few weeks' time, she had no time for leisurely speculation.

Events had been so attention-consuming, she found, that she hardly had time to do much of anything other than spend her mornings planning details of the wedding with Jana and Marian, and then go to work in the afternoons. In the evenings she was about ready to drop into her bed without supper, she was so exhausted. After much discussion, she had decided that she would try to keep her job, and this meant taking leave from work for a honeymoon. It created much dismay in her head nurse and a terrific amount of juggling on the work schedule. The time off was approved, however, and Katherine liked to think that it was because she was such a good worker, but she didn't mention so to anyone else.

Perhaps the absorption in the whirling and hectic events made her let down her guard. Perhaps the fast-moving days trickling by and the frantic rush to get the business squared up for the honeymoon had made Luke just a bit lax too. Perhaps the passage of time without any action from James had lulled her into a false sense of security, or maybe it was just that her mind did not work in such devious patterns as his did. Whatever the reason, she did not suspect a thing when Luke phoned her from his office late one afternoon.

'Katie-bug, I can't pick you up this afternoon, I'm afraid,' he told her regretfully. 'I've had the Ferrari garaged this afternoon. There's something wrong with it. The mechanic says that it shouldn't be too serious, though. I'm going to put in an extra couple of hours at the office while I wait. Is Jana still at the hospital?'

'No,' she answered, a bit puzzled. 'As far as I know, she left at the normal time. Why'd you think she was here?'

'I rang home to see if she could pick you up, and no one answered,' he replied. 'Do you know where she could have gone?'

'It's Marian's day off,' she said after a moment's reflection. 'I'll bet you that they went shopping for the afternoon, or popped out to the grocery store to get something for supper. You know, I bet that is it. Jana hates to cook anything if she can possibly get away with it, and we're going to have frozen pizza, or something equally revolting.'

'No doubt,' he said with a little laugh. 'Well, do you have enough money with you for a taxi? It will get dull after a couple of hours if you were to wait for me at the hospital, I'm afraid.'

'No problem,' she said. 'I've enough with me. I wouldn't want to wait around here, anyway. I keep dreaming about that lovely bottle of wine chilling in the fridge, and I can't wait to get home. You'll find me in a blissful state, no doubt, with the bottle empty and rolling under the couch while I snooze on top. At least I won't remember how the frozen pizza tastes.'

'You drink that whole bottle, my love, and I'll take my share of it out of your hide,' she was told in no uncertain terms. She laughed and told him that she might save him a glass if he was good, and they rang off.

She didn't suspect a thing until she stepped out on to the kerb just outside the hospital at exactly five minutes past-five, her usual meeting time with Luke, and found that she had to wait for the taxi she'd called some ten minutes ago. Watching the left side of the street, as she presumed the direction of the cab's arrival to be, since it was from this direction that the semicircle for the pick up of passengers started, she was considerably surprised at the polite tap on her right shoulder. When she turned to see who it was, she turned white.

'Miss Farlough?' the big, dark man, the one who had bumped into her in the restaurant some weeks ago, spoke quietly. She blinked and took a quick step back. He did not bother to move. She took his measure in a glance and found time to reflect bitterly that he wouldn't have to move to block her puny response. He looked perfectly capable of catching her even if she had been half a block away, and she was no slow mover.

'What do you want?' she asked sharply, taking a quick, comprehensive glance around. There weren't any people about, as she met Luke in front of the hospital and most of the staff went round the back way to a private car park.

The man just smiled. 'Why, Miss Farlough, I don't want anything,' he told her pleasantly. 'But your father wants you. Would you be so good as to step this way?'

'And,' she asked, looking directly into his eyes, 'what if I don't?' There was the dark saloon car close by, and she could see the back of another person's head, in the driving position.

'Then I suppose I'll have to hit you in the jaw,' was his reply. He was balanced on the balls of his feet, for all his air of relaxation, just like she had seen Luke balance once. It was a dangerous sight. She took another good look around her, and found that there was no one about, not even across the street. There would be no witnesses. 'Have you decided which it is to be?' he asked.

'You do,' she told him drily, 'pick your moments.' With complete composure, she moved forward of her own accord to step into the car with the assistance of his helping hand. It would have been futile to do otherwise.

He climbed into the back seat with her, and without a word from the driver, the car shot forward to pull into the traffic's flow. She stared at the back of the driver's head for a moment with a surge of recognition.

'Of course!' she said calmly. 'How are you doing, Joss?' The head jerked a little.

Joss's hateful, insinuating voice flowed back to her. 'I'm just fine, Miss Farlough. In fact, everybody is doing just fine. Might I add that you're going to find Mr Farlough very healthy.' He added nastily, 'You might even find him, er, forgiving, but I wouldn't necessarily count on it.'

'I don't believe that I'll hold my breath,' she told him mildly. This contained statement had his sharp eyes flicking to her reflection in the rearview mirror with some surprise. She caught this and had to hide a smile. Despite her discomfiture, and uneasy apprehension at the forthcoming interview with a man she'd give anything to be able to forget, she had managed to show a shell of composure that she'd cultivated in the recent past. Always in the past Joss could be assured of some kind of agitated response from his malicious digs, and the mere mention of James's displeasure would have been enough to send the former Katherine into the grip of fear.

In a way, the composure that she maintained outwardly was not just a shell. Deep inside herself, Katherine had found a measure of the strength that Luke had prophesied was in her, and with the strength came peace of mind. She was worried and, yes, to herself she admitted some degree of apprehension. But underneath all these surface agitations there ran a deep flowing river of serenity. She was not the same girl who had been cowed into submission all her life. James was, she thought grimly, going to be surprised.

She spared no glances for the rather menacing aspect of the man sitting so quietly beside her. His slightly battered visage was still familiar in some way, but she did not trouble herself to try to put his face to a memory. He did not matter to her existence beyond the fact that he was a restriction for the moment. One thing she did notice, though, was that the jacket he was wearing did not fit as exactly as it could. She had no doubt that there was a gun somewhere on his formidable person.

When they pulled up the long, shady driveway to her old home, she spared an admiring glance for the new electronic apparatus attached to the double gates. They swished shut behind the car, and she began to know a moment of disquiet.

She presented an unruffled calm though, as she thanked the stranger politely when he opened the car door for her. His eyes flickered but he showed no sign other than this, and she had not been looking at him anyway. Joss had not spared the unobtrusive man a single look.

The front door opened as they all mounted the steps, and she lifted her eyes to look into the eyes of a beast. 'Hello, James,' she said, as if she were coming home after an afternoon's shopping, 'how've you been?'

'Very well, thank you,' he replied in the same vein, his expression enough to make her want to scream. She had lost capacity to feel the incredible impact that his cold and utterly inhuman face could have on her. 'And yourself?'

'In good health.' In the spacious hall, she stopped to see where he would direct her. He indicated with one hand the room that in an earlier day had been called the drawing-room, but was now a huge family-type den. Its windows overlooked the front gardens and driveway, and let in the morning sun. The décor was tasteful; James had hired the best decorator in the area. With a calm grace, she moved forward to drop suddenly to one knee as a vicious hand whistled just by her head. Putting out a steady hand to balance herself, she waited for a moment, crouched where she had fallen as she observed her father's actions. She had not been surprised by the blow. It was a favourite trick of his to hit out when he thought his victim was least suspecting, and she had seen his calculation of the distance and position a split second before he had struck out.

Joss was already going down the hall and hadn't seen the encounter. The stranger, who had stopped just inside the front door had not moved an inch from his rigid position, and he stared ahead of him with blank eyes, but Katherine caught a glimpse of a muscle in his jaw twitching. With a slightly raised eyebrow, she asked her father, 'Do you suppose I can get up now, or would you rather kick me around a bit first?' Her tone, almost amused, and also her swift response to his attempted blow had his light, merciless eyes staring at her in blank surprise.

He recovered almost immediately, though, and with a charming smile that had her privately wishing she could afford the luxury of retching he said, 'By all means, my pet, do pick yourself up from that sprawl.' He sounded, she observed, almost disdainfully elegant.

With the same swift grace that had sent her down, she swung to her feet and preceded him into the family room. She stopped just inside the door. 'May I sit?'

'Do feel free to, my dear,' he replied cordially. He watched her sit down and observed her face for several moments in a disconcerting way. The man who had approached her in the street had followed them silently into the room, and he posted himself at the other side of the door. His presence, so superficially unobtrusive and totally ignored, made her look at him in speculation. He was like a piece of furniture, James accorded him as much attention, and must have been with him for some time to be treated with such implicit trust.

James moved to a comfortable chair and seated himself with a flick to his immaculate slacks. With barely a glance to the dark man, he said carelessly, 'Mike, pour us a drink, will you? What will you have, Katherine?'

She answered promptly, 'A rum and Coke, please, with a lime twist.'

Her father added to this, 'And I'll have a gin on the rocks.'

He turned his head to look at Katherine. 'I find Michael a delight, my dear. He's been amazingly resourceful, you know, and has been watching you from the moment you left this house.' A slight clatter accompanied his words and she looked at the man who had impressed her as being so deft, as he bent to pick up the lid to the ice bucket that he'd dropped. His eyes met hers intently. For some bizarre reason she felt he was trying to send her a wordless message.

'Really?' she murmured, with a delicately raised brow. The man called Mike dropped his eyes, and she turned her gaze to her father. He had been busy watching her and had not seen the exchange. For some odd reason she refrained from mentioning that she had seen him before and contented herself with saying, 'You've been busy.'

'Yes,' said James with perfect satisfaction. Mike, behind his back, gave her a very slight nod. She took this in with absolutely no change of expression, not even the bat of an eye, and when the dark man came forward to place her drink in her hands, she didn't even raise her eyes to his, receiving the drink in silence.

After sipping their drinks for a few minutes, their light conversation was interrupted by Mike interposing a quickly whispered message into James's ear. Pausing to nod at him, James spared him a quick glance and a brief, 'Good, but be quick about it and come right back.' The man left the room, moving like a panther stalking its prey, with infinite grace. When he had left, James said lightly, 'I believe that Elizabeth will have supper ready by seven, so that leaves us with just enough time to have a good talk, don't you think? We have a few things to get straight between us, just a few points, pet, and then with the air sufficiently cleared we should be able to enjoy a nice meal.'

Her attention caught in the greying light by the sight of a man loping off down the driveway had him turning his head and looking out briefly. 'Mike has turned out to be a veritable treasure. He is indispensable, and, I hope, willing to be of some use to me in the future. I hired him shortly before you left. At the time I had no idea that he would prove to be so valuable. He's gone to check on the electronic gates—his own idea—to make sure everything's secure for the night, and should be back any moment.'

Katherine had been puzzling over in her mind the events of the afternoon and had many uneasy questions to ask, so she brushed this aside quickly. 'Tell me,' she asked, 'did you lure Marian and Jana out of the house this afternoon?'

'Yes,' he said calmly. 'Don't worry, pet, they should be getting home any minute now. We took the housekeeper when she left the house this afternoon, and deposited her some distance away and made her phone, er, Jana to tell her precisely what we wished her to. With no idea of subterfuge, Jana took off to pick up her precious housekeeper and to see about getting a tow truck for the "flat tyre". They were both quite busy, while Joss tinkered with Dalton's car. It was all amazingly simple, but rather impromptu as I decided to move only this afternoon. Joss and Mike have had quite a busy time of it. They had no idea that they were to have such a diverting couple of hours. I must say, they make quite a team.'

'I see.' During this willingly given explanation, Mike had once again slipped into the room to stand against the inside wall, just by the cocktail cabinet. Katherine, in spite of herself, had begun to feel something close to panic.

'Now, then,' said James after a moment, 'let's start talking about the future. I see a beautiful ring on your left hand, pet. Take it off. It should be quite an expressive message to Dalton.'

'No,' she said, clenching her hand into a tight fist.

'Mike,' James ordered calmly, 'take the ring off her

finger.' Mike started obediently forward and halted just before her. His dark eyes once again stared into hers intently. She got that same feeling: What, she thought in great perplexity, is he trying to say to me?

'May I have the ring, Miss Farlough?' he asked her, again as polite as before. 'Don't make me have to use force.'

She said grimly, 'You'll have to break my hand to get it off. I came with you this afternoon because I could see no choice in the matter: you would have had me in that car with or without my consent, and I preferred to be alert instead of knocked unconscious. Don't estimate me by that incident. This is something I won't allow! You'll probably have the ring sooner or later, but I won't give in.' She saw him briefly close his eyes and on inspiration, on a crazy, unfounded hunch, she held out her clenched fist to him as if in invitation. 'Here, try it. You may be stronger, but I promise you, nobody beats me for stubbornness!'

The man called Mike didn't move.

CHAPTER TEN

AFTER just a second, James sat disdainfully, 'Hold on a moment, Mike. She means what she says, and I don't have the time or the inclination to put up with this nonsense.' The big man before her relaxed slightly, his face clearing almost imperceptibly of its cloud. Katherine watched him quietly as he took his place back against the wall. James had not noticed anything out of the ordinary. With a contemplative stare at her rather white face, he leaned back in his chair in an attitude of ease, saying lightly, 'There are other methods of persuasion, I'm sure, that will get us further along, with very little fuss. Pet, you've become fond of the people you have stayed with, have you not?'

Her gaze moved warily from Mike's impassive face to her father's. 'They've been good to me,' she replied without expression. A thread of apprehension shot through her; James wore a particularly speculative look as he perused her immobile face. It was a look she'd seen before, the look of a snake about to strike its victim, the look of a hunter inspecting its prey.

'You must feel some measure of, ah, affection for Dalton,' he mused slowly. 'I'm persuaded that although you are a foolish girl, you are not quite stupid. Do you know what could happen to someone on an empty road at night if a tyre blows? People have died in such accidents. Or, perhaps a tragic accident at home, maybe a faulty electrical wire bursting into flames in the middle of the night, when everyone is asleep. Do you understand what I am saying, pet?'

Those animal-like eyes watched her as if she were some pathetic insect squirming feebly at the end of a pin.

'Why are you doing this?' she asked him quietly, with the same deadly calm as before. There was a subtle difference now, though. There was a quality of violence in her eyes that had not been evident throughout the encounter.

'Why?' he asked, as if puzzled by the question. 'Yes, indeed, why? Because Dalton took something I wanted. I am referring to the choice warehouse property a few months ago, in case you hadn't remembered. But that has nothing to do with this; he'll be taken care of later on this evening by a few well-placed items in those warehouses, illegal, of course, and a quiet anonymous phone call to the police. That will take care of my business score with him. It might even be the catalyst for the quiet sale of the buildings in dispute, who knows? But as far as you're concerned, why, he took something of mine without asking—you, pet—and I find that I want you back. And you will stay, for if you don't, as sure as if you had signed their death warrants, your friends will die.'

Such a feeling of revulsion and rage swept over her at these dispassionate words that she sat, a blaze kindling and growing in her mind at this speech. This was such evil, she thought, such unadulterated venom that it just can't be borne ... With no warning, with incredible speed and surprising accuracy, she stood swiftly and in one fluid motion threw her heavy glass right at her father's smiling face. Neither he nor Mike had time to react before the half-empty glass smashed across his left cheekbone with a painful-sounding thump. Liquid was spilt all over the plush, off-white carpet. The glass fell in three pieces, a thin trickle of

red slid down James's whitened face, and then he
launched out of his chair and came for her with the
most terrifying expression of rage she had ever seen.

She had time to back several paces away, shrinking
from his cruel, furious, biting hands which fastened on
her slim shoulders, when suddenly a very large object
catapulted into the room through the french windows,
splintering glass flying everywhere in a glittering
shower of light, and hurtled towards James.

Events after that seemed to jumble in Katherine's
mind like clips from a newsreel catching separate,
unconnected scenes of a momentous occasion. She
remembered her surprise at Mike's smiling stillness at
the intruder's attack, after he had jerked involuntarily
her way when her father had grabbed her; she
remembered Luke's incredible, wrathful onslaught at
James's unprepared back, and how her father had gone
down like a ton of bricks; she remembered after being
pushed back and told unceremoniously to get out of
the way how she sank into a corner chair, shaken and
bruised, to watch the proceedings. She couldn't seem
to get a clear image of what was happening between
Luke and James, for they were thrashing about far
too much for that, but she very definitely had time to
wonder at Mike's marked lack of participation when
Joss and an apparently hastily summoned groom
crashed into the room. After a stunned moment, Joss
picked up a large brass ornament like a club and bore
down on Luke, who was momentarily on top of James
presenting an exposed neck, and there was a sudden
crack that made her jump as if she had been lashed
with a whip.

She watched Joss drop the brass ornament with a
cry, and clutch at his shoulder. The groom, extremely
bewildered, made a quick unrestrained movement as
he stared across the room in astonishment, and she

turned her head to see Mike's smiling, warning shake of the head as he pointed a hand gun straight at the other man. She stared, much like the groom had done, with her pretty mouth hanging open at this unexpected sight.

Luke stood up from her father's inert figure, breathing heavily and brushed his tousled hair off his forehead to grin at Mike's unruffled appearance. 'You sure know how to exert yourself,' he commented acidly, making Mike's own smile widen. Luke turned to Katherine and said to her placidly, 'Shut your mouth, love, you're catching flies,' which had the effect of making her mouth close with a decided snap. He turned to survey the ruined room with a raised eyebrow, just as in the far distance a few sirens could be heard wailing. 'I was, perhaps a bit precipitate, but I think under the circumstances, it was understandable. The police should understand, don't you think, old boy?' This was addressed to Joss, who was by now crouched on the floor and inspecting the red on his fingers.

Katherine's calm, which had not deserted her through the whole unbelievable scene, quite fled at the sight of the small amount of blood, and with a hiccup she buried her face in her hands and started to cry. There were exclamations, and quickly snapped-out orders, and Luke was pulling her out of her seat to lead her gently from the room. In the hall, he sternly admonished a small cluster of the household staff to disperse until otherwise notified and he took her to the bottom of the stairs where she sank down gratefully. He sat beside her and put his strong arm round her, making her lean against his shoulder. After a shuddering moment, she pushed his arm away and sat up straight.

'I'm fine—no, I really am,' she said to his

unbelieving stare, 'It's just the sight of the blood, it—sort of sparked off some memories and I felt a bit queasy for a minute.' Uniformed men were coming through the front door and moving with precise efficiency into the other room, but neither Katherine nor Luke paid them any heed. 'What I am is very confused,' she told him and watched him smile. 'Who is Mike?'

'He's a private investigator who I hired the week of the dinner party,' Luke told her with a thread of amusement in his voice. 'I—let's say I just had my suspicions about your father's good intentions, and I knew he couldn't do anything legal to harm me, so I was left with some rather uneasy apprehensions.'

She stared. 'I don't understand,' she stammered. 'How did you get suspicious? Why did you think that James would do anything illegal? How do I fit into all this? I'm sorry, maybe I'm just feeling a little slow, but I'm not understanding this much.'

'Eli Parson, a tired and thoroughly honourable old gentleman, had a long talk with me when he privately sold me those choice water-front warehouses,' Luke told her patiently. 'He knew that I wanted to convert the site into a large exclusive hotel complex, and yet was unable to bid as high as your father was prepared to go for the property. He told me that he would far rather that I had the property than James, because he'd had a suspicion for some time that your father was dealing in illegal drug activities, and Parson emphatically told me that he didn't want any property of his to go for that purpose.'

She raised her two hands to cover her mouth, feeling sick. 'Oh, no,' she whispered, 'I had absolutely no idea.'

A steadying hand clasped her shoulder. 'I'm afraid so, love,' he murmured sympathetically. 'That's why

James was so furious at not being allowed to purchase the water-front property. The location would have been ideal for shipments, and he had been waiting for years to get his hands on just such an exclusive bit of property. And when I found you, a present that heaven dropped into my lap, and was told by you in no uncertain terms that James had unsavoury plans for me, I decided to keep Mike on the job. Your father then made some nasty threats to me the day you left home, and he made some, ah, shall I just say unhappy comments about you that had me a touch on the look-out for trouble.'

She asked him curiously, 'Why does Mike seem so familiar to me? It seems fairly easy for he and I to have just missed paths, since he was coming and I was going.'

'He probably looked familiar to you because the night of the party, he was playing bartender and handed you two whiskys,' Luke replied whimsically. 'And I was never sure if you had seen us one day when you and I took a walk. Remember? You did manage to get a glimpse of his back as he hurried away, and I told you that he was a neighbour.'

Comprehension dawned. 'Of course! How could I have been so stupid?' she asked herself disgustedly. 'I've been racking my brain as to why he looked so familiar, and couldn't for the life of me remember!'

'And a good thing it was, too!' an emphatic voice spoke beside them feelingly. 'We were counting on you not remembering.' They both looked round at Mike, who was leaning against the staircase railing. People milled about and voices were trying to talk over each other, but the commotion was completely outside the little world composed of the three. 'You gave me a few bad moments this afternoon,' he continued in his pleasant voice, shaking his dark head. 'When you looked at me so coolly this afternoon as if you were trying to decide whether or not to put my threat to the test, I was breaking out in a sweat for fear I really would have to knock you in the jaw, to look authentic in front of Joss! And when you told me I'd have to break your hand to get your ring, I was literally trembling! I couldn't have brought myself to do that and was afraid that my cover was to be blown too soon. Your father unexpectedly saved us from an uncomfortable situation. I had just tensed myself to jump on him and knock him out when he told me to forget it for the time being.'

'Did you really tell him that?' Luke asked her with a soft laugh. 'I think I've got more than I bargained for when I asked you to marry me! You have, my love, a frightening accuracy and a powerful throwing arm. Do you throw things often when you lose your temper?'

'Actually,' she murmured, blushing furiously, 'this is the first time I've ever done it. I quite surprised myself.'

'And everyone else,' Mike said with admiration. 'I was about to pull him off you when Luke burst on to the scene with such a dramatic entrance. I was a bit disappointed in my thwarted intentions! I had wanted to rescue the damsel in distress, you see.'

'Huh!' Luke snorted. 'She's my damsel, and I'll thank you to remember that I do the rescuing for her and no one else. By the way, why didn't you get hold of me sooner? Kate wasn't supposed to be involved in any of this.'

Mike looked embarrassed. 'I didn't find out that we were to execute an abduction until about half an hour before we had to set everything up. James sent Joss and me after your housekeeper and I wasn't alone all afternoon to phone you. Sorry about that.'

'Forget it,' Luke told him. 'I at least had the satisfaction of knowing that she wasn't in real danger.'

'That's rich!' she exploded in a surprising burst of anger. 'And I was left in the dark to imagine all sorts of things. I must thank you for that, mustn't I?' She glared at the two men with such ferocity that Mike blinked and Luke's smile straightened immediately. 'Why couldn't you have let me in on the secret? You could at least have told me that the person trailing me was a friend and not a foe! It's no wonder that I'm a nervous wreck.'

'You could have fooled me,' Mike muttered, at which statement she turned and glared him into silence. Luke's grin had started to deepen again.

'But, love,' he said to her gently, 'we were planning on scotching at the beginning any plans your father was to put into action. You were to have been quite unaware of the situation. Besides, what would have happened if James had decided to have someone else instead of Mike make a move on you? We had to leave you alert and suspicious for your own safety. I was,' he continued at her determined glare, 'trying to save you any further pain at your father's hands.' This had her eyes misting with unexpected tears, and she put out a hand to have it grasped tightly.

'But how,' she asked when she had her composure back, 'did you manage to get here so fast if Mike didn't let you know what was going on?'

'Deduction,' he answered succinctly, 'and an unexpected visit at the office from a very ruffled Marian and an apparently incoherent sister. I was literally fuming at the gates when Mike came out and turned off the electricity to let me in.'

Her eyes met Mike's in comprehension. 'Checking to see if the gates were secure!' she exclaimed. She looked back at Luke. 'Then you were outside the window nearly the whole time.'

'Yes,' he admitted, playing with her fingers absently, 'but as the windows were closed I couldn't hear what was said. I can only hope that James had enough time to spill enough evidence for Mike to testify against him.'

'Spill enough!' Mike exclaimed. 'He confessed to just about everything in connection with you, Luke, apart from kidnapping charges. I'm sure that the "illegal items" he was going to have planted in your warehouses are the drugs we've been trying to find, and I'll bet you that they're hidden somewhere in the stables. He mentioned something of that sort to me this afternoon. He's hanged himself with what he told me and Katherine. When the police question her——'

The warning glance Luke shot him was too late to have effect, and Mike stopped in the middle of the declaration to look in dismay from one to the other. 'What did I say wrong?'

Katherine had not missed the exchange of glances, and she answered stiffly, 'Nothing, Mike. Luke, don't look at him like that! It's quite all right. I mean to testify against James.' At this calm declaration, she put her head in her hands for the second time that evening and started to cry, not, as she tried to tell Luke through her tears, for the father she was losing, but for the father she'd never had.

After she had managed to calm herself and had the chance to splash water on her face, a hesitant approach from a police sergeant had her readily answering his questions. This went on for quite some time, she sitting on the bottom stair while the police officer jotted down her replies to his questions and found that her story was confirming Mike Carradine's exactly, and was broken only by the exit of her father. He was handcuffed and escorted by two policemen, and he stopped in the hall to stand for a minute very still, looking at her with those empty eyes. She stared back for a long-drawn-out moment and took in his attitude of coldness, the absence of any remorse or affection in his eyes. Then, with complete composure and deliberation, she turned back to answer one of the officer's questions. She did not watch him leave his home.

Finally, with a close look at her too-brilliant eyes and tense attitude after a long period of questioning, Luke entered quietly into the conversation and put an end to the sergeant's questions, saying politely that he would be glad to come to the police station in the morning with Miss Farlough for further questioning, and to sign a written statement, but that she was too tired for any more that night. The burly officer took one look at Katherine's over-excited tenseness, and silently agreed. He bowed himself out.

Soon, she was bundled into Jana's car and Luke was driving home. When he would have got out of the car after they had arrived, she stopped him with a quick hand on his arm.

'Please,' she murmured. He subsided back into his seat and regarded her with a question in his eyes. She watched him carefully, the question she wanted to ask had been bothering her for some time, and she found that she could no longer wait to ask it. She dropped her eyes. 'You once told me,' she said with some difficulty, 'that you would always answer any question I asked you. Would you answer one for me now?'

'You know I will,' was his grave response.

She stared ahead of her and took a deep breath. The question came out in a terrific rush, 'Are you having second thoughts about marrying me?'

In comparison, his reply seemed ages in coming. When it finally did, she closed her eyes with the pain of it. 'Yes, I am.'

She clenched her hands into tight fists to bear the coming blows, and said jerkily, 'I—thought as much. You've been acting with such reserve lately that I . . .' She turned and looked at him, surprising a look of such deep pain on his face that she reached out and quickly squeezed his hand, continuing with some difficulty, 'It's all right. Tell me truthfully, would you—have you found that you'd prefer not getting married after all?'

'It's not what I want,' he said and paused, so that she completely misunderstood what he was trying to say. The pain was so bad, that she bent forward for a moment, with her hands holding on to the dashboard.

'I see.' In spite of her efforts, her voice wobbled horribly. 'Do you want your ring back?'

'I hadn't finished,' he said, and she heard the strain in his voice. A silence, and then, 'You seem—eager to give it back. Could it be that you've changed your mind?'

'No!' she burst out. She strove to get herself in control. 'But if you have, then I won't, I mean I don't want to stand in your way, if you no longer want to get married. I—I want you to be happy, and you haven't seemed very happy lately, and I was just wondering if you didn't want . . . oh, hell.' Her voice trailed away miserably.

Her hand was taken in one of his hard grips and squeezed until she opened her eyes to look at him. His head was leaning back against the headrest, and he was staring up at the car's roof, smiling. 'I love you, Katie-bug,' he said tenderly. She sagged in her seat, immeasurably relieved.

She whispered to him, 'I love you,' and felt his hand tighten.

'You see,' he said quietly, 'I was beginning to worry that perhaps we were rushing things a bit, and I was starting to doubt whether it was such a good thing for us to marry so quickly. You know, I'm not really a knight in shining armour, Katie-love, although you make a very beautiful damsel in distress. I'm human and I have faults and I especially have weaknesses. One of my worries was that because I was the first male that ever showed any interest in you for yourself that you would fancy yourself in love with me, later on realising your mistake. By then it might have been too late. I wanted to give you the chance to get away before either of us got too hurt. It's not what I want, but what you want.'

'You crazy nut,' was all she could get out for a minute. Then, in a stronger voice, she continued, 'You've always told me to trust you. Well, trust is a two-way street in a relationship. I thank you for your trust in my judgment of my own feelings! I've met plenty of men, I'll have you know, even if I am a lot younger than you! I know what I want all right, and as soon as you realise that I want you, then I'm sure that we'll get along very amicably. But,' and she tugged her hand out of his suddenly, 'until you just put yourself out on a limb, then I guess we won't ever know, will we? Excuse me, I'm going inside.' She jumped out of the car and started running for the house.

A car door slammed and footsteps ran after her. She increased her pace, loping for the house as fast as she could, one part of her registering with satisfaction that he was coming after her very fast and about to overtake her. That was good. She hoped that her little outburst of pseudo-anger would shake him up enough to realise that he had to trust her as much as she trusted him to make the relationship work. Two hands on her waist jerked her round, and she was hauled into his arms roughly. With her head pushed down on his chest, she could feel his pulse racing with deep throbs.

He heaved a huge sigh and tightened his arms, putting his face down to bury it in her hair. That also was good. It was the best feeling she'd ever experienced, to have the man she loved show her evidence of his need for her. She put her arms around his waist. It would be all right now, she knew. He had reached a point where he loved her so much that he would just have to take her on faith. Time, and a lot of demonstrative loving would show him that what she felt would last.

'I'm sorry, Katie-bug,' he murmured, moving his face in her thick soft hair as if he loved to feel it on his face.'It's just that you had been so unsure of what you wanted out of life until just recently, and I wanted to make sure you weren't making a mistake.'

'I'm an adult, Luke,' her voice was muffled in his shoulder as she spoke. Hidden from his eyes, she smiled.

'I know, sweet.'

'I like to think that I've been making the right decisions since I left home,' she continued, enjoying herself hugely.

'You have. You've grown so much, and I'm so proud of you. Kate, turn your face to me,' he commanded, a thread of unsteadiness running in his tone. No longer smiling, she complied instantly and his mouth came down fiercely to crush hers. Soon her pulse was racing as hard and as unsteadily as his. 'I need you so much, my love,' he whispered, 'that I was just afraid.'

'Hush, you silly man. I need you, too.'

Some time later, a very long time later, as Jana was putting the last batch of chocolate chip cookies into the oven to bake, in the cosy kitchen the huge calico cat that had been napping just under the warm stove looked up and blinked sleepily. She had just registered this when a deep, amused voice spoke behind her and made her shriek. She whirled and looked at Luke standing just behind her with his arm possessively around a flushed and radiantly lovely Katherine. Both were grinning with what she felt to be a ridiculous amount of enjoyment from her reaction. She snapped, 'Lucas Trevor Dalton, you've been sneaking up behind me for years and scaring the living daylights out of me! I put my foot down at this! If you don't stop that detestable habit, I don't care how big you are, I'll take a fly-swatter to your bottom, like I used to!' Her irate expression began to fade, and a twinkle showed in the blue of her eyes. She held out a plate to Katherine. 'Have a cookie, love. *He* doesn't get any.'

'Well, Katie-bug,' he said with deep satisfaction, snatching a cookie before Jana could jerk the plate away. 'It looks like we're home.' Disturbed from her nap, Matilda the Monster swished her tail and slunk disdainfully away.

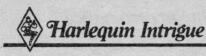

Harlequin Intrigue

Two exciting new stories each month.

Each title mixes a contemporary, sophisticated romance with the surprising twists and turns of a puzzler... romance with "something more."

Because romance can be quite an adventure.

Romance, Suspense and Adventure

Harlequin Presents

Coming Next Month

Available in January wherever paperback books are sold, or through Harlequin Reader Service:

In the U.S.
901 Fuhrmann Blvd.
P.O. Box 1397
Buffalo, N.Y. 14240-1397

In Canada
P.O. Box 603
Fort Erie, Ontario
L2A 5X3

ATTRACTIVE, SPACE SAVING BOOK RACK

Display your most prized novels on this handsome and sturdy book rack. The hand-rubbed walnut finish will blend into your library decor with quiet elegance, providing a practical organizer for your favorite hard-or soft-covered books.

Only $9.95

Approximately 16" x 8" when assembled

Assembles in seconds!

To order, rush your name, address and zip code, along with a check or money order for $10.70* ($9.95 plus 75¢ postage and handling) payable to *Harlequin Reader Service*:

Harlequin Reader Service
Book Rack Offer
901 Fuhrmann Blvd.
P.O. Box 1396
Buffalo, NY 14269-1396

Offer not available in Canada.

BKR-1A

*New York and Iowa residents add appropriate sales tax.

Step into a world of pulsing adventure, gripping emotion and lush sensuality with these evocative love stories penned by today's best-selling authors in the highest romantic tradition. Pursuing their passionate dreams against a backdrop of the past's most colorful and dramatic moments, our vibrant heroines and dashing heroes will make history come alive for you.

Watch for two new Harlequin Historicals each month, available wherever Harlequin books are sold. History was never so much fun—you won't want to miss a single moment!